PORT APHRODITE

Little Sister came to New Venusberg.

Grimes was not sorry that the voyage was over. Prunella sat with him in the control cab as he eased the pinnace down to Port Aphrodite. She took him to task for evincing interest in the chalk giantess that, viewed from the air, was a huge advertisement for the major entertainment for sale on New Venusberg.

Cut out from the green turf she was, although the two white hillocks that were her breasts, the oval blue ponds that were her eyes must have been artificial. There was golden hair on the head and above the jointure of the thighs (a flowering creeper, Grimes later discovered) and her nipples (marked by a sort of lichen) were pink.

"If you were as much interested in me as you seem to be in that thing," said Prunella, "you might be of some use."

"I'm getting my bearings," said Grimes.

A. BERTRAM CHANDLER
has written these DAW books:

THE BIG BLACK MARK

STAR COURIER

TO KEEP THE SHIP

THE FAR TRAVELER

THE BROKEN CYCLE

STAR LOOT

THE ANARCH LORDS

THE WAY BACK

MATILDA'S STEPCHILDREN

A. Bertram Chandler

DAW BOOKS, INC.
DONALD A. WOLLHEIM, PUBLISHER

1633 Broadway, New York, NY 10019

To Matilda—long may she waltz!

FIRST DAW PRINTING, JULY 1983

1   2   3   4   5   6   7   8   9

DAW TRADEMARK REGISTERED
U.S. PAT. OFF. MARCA
REGISTRADA. HECHO EN U.S.A.

PRINTED IN U.S.A.

One

Fenella Pruin did not like Grimes.

Grimes did not like Fenella Pruin.

Their *de jure* relationship was that of charterer's representative and Owner/Master of the vessel under charter. Their *de facto* relationship was that of employer and servant. Grimes, bound by the terms of the charter party did as he was told and Miss Pruin did the telling. He did not like it. She, most obviously, did.

It was a charter that he would never have accepted had he not been so desperately in need of money. But he had been grounded on Bronsonia with port dues mounting steadily, with heavy fines still to pay and with the salvage award in respect of the obsolescent, renamed Epsilon Class freighter *Bronson Star* still being haggled over by the lawyers. The other *Bronson Star*, a newspaper, had come to his financial rescue. This *Bronson Star* was a sensational rag which also owned trivi stations and the like. Although its sales on its home planet were not small it derived the bulk of its considerable income from syndicated material. It had earned, over the years, a reputation as the galaxy's premier muckraker. It employed a highly efficient team of scavengers; the material that they gathered was, after processing, syndicated to every world with a human population and to quite a few planets whose inhabitants, although non-human, enjoyed salacity.

Chief of the muckrakers was Fenella Pruin. Normally she followed her long nose to savoury (in a perverted sense of the word) dirt by taking passage to likely places in regular spaceliners. But now and again she had found it impossible to get away, at extremely short notice, from worlds upon which she had endeared herself to prominent citizens by her snooping. On occasion she has been considerably roughed up. Twice she had been jailed on trumped up charges and her extrication from prison had been expensive to her employers back on Bronsonia. (She hadn't been murdered yet—but, Grimes of-

5

ten thought during the voyage, there has to be a first time for everything.)

So *The Bronson Star* had chartered Grimes' deep space pinnace *Little Sister*. They were, to a certain extent, killing two birds with one stone. Not only would their Miss Pruin be taken to where she wished to go—and whisked away therefrom as soon as things got sticky—but Grimes' own name would help to sell the material garnered by the notorious news hen. He, too, had achieved a certain notoriety which might well be of value to others if not to himself.

Miss Pruin was travelling under a *nom de guerre*. According to the documentation provided by her employers—and they had done a very thorough job—she was Prunella Fenn, a spinster schoolteacher whose life had been changed when her loving pupils gave her, as birthday present, a ticket in the annual super lottery, the Bronson Bonanza. Fantastically she had won the astronomical first prize. According to news items in specially printed isues of *The Bronson Star*—which had been placed aboard *Little Sister* before lift off—the sudden influx of great wealth had gone to the fictitious Miss Fenn's head. She had started to make up for lost time. From prim schoolmarm she had made the transition to good time girl. Finding Bronsonia too dull for her—and that wouldn't have been hard, thought Grimes sourly, as he read the spurious press reports so as to acquaint himself with his passenger's cover story—she had charted *Little Sister* for a galactic tour, with a first stop at New Venusberg.

He looked at the photographs accompanying some of the newspaper articles. There was one of himself among them. *The famous Captain John Grimes* . . . he read. That photographer had made him look all pipe and ears. *The famous Captain John Grimes, hero of the* Discovery *mutiny and of the* Bronson Star *affair, whose fabulous golden spaceyacht* Little Sister *has been chartered by lucky lady Prunella Fenn* . . .

Then there was lucky lady Prunella Fenn herself, labelled "the golden schoolmarm." The photographer had flattered *her*. (Probably it had been more than his job was worth to do otherwise). The portrait was of a slim, darkhaired (before making changes to her appearance Fenella Pruin had been carroty) with slightly protrusive (another attempt at disguise) front teeth, with rather too much nose (although that organ was thin and almost aristocratic) and rather too little chin. She looked like an intelligent ferret, although a quite attractive one. She looked far more attractive in the photograph than she was in actuality.

She interrupted his studies by yelling in her shrill soprano, "Grimes, what about a drink? After all the money I've paid to charter this tub of yours I'm entitled to some pretense of service!"

All the money you've *paid*? thought Grimes resentfully. Nonetheless he got up from his seat, went aft into the tiny galley, busied himself with bottles and glasses. He did not have to ask her what she wished. Her taste in potables never changed. He put a small ice cube into a large glass which he filled with brandy. He decided that it would be bad manners—not that *she* ever worried about manners—to let her drink alone. His choice was pink gin—heavy on the liquor, very easy on the ice. Normally he drank very little alcohol while in space but Fenella Pruin—correction: Prunella Fenn—was driving him to it.

She was curled up in an inflatable easy chair in front of the playmaster. She had brought a large supply of her own spools with her. Her tastes ran to what Grimes thought of as boring porn. In the screen an actor and actress made up to resemble (vaguely) Hindu deities had gotten themselves into an intricate tangle of organs and slowly writhing limbs. The really boring part was the commentary, couched in allegedly poetic language.

She took her drink from him without thanks, downed half of it in one gulp. Grimes sipped from his, but not slowly. She swallowed the rest of her brandy, indicated that she needed a refill. He got one for her. In the screen the heterosexual lovers were replaced by two naked, teen-aged girls. The accompanying commentary was no improvement on what had gone before.

Emboldened by gin Grimes asked, "Don't you think that we might have some of my spools for a change? I've some good adventure stories . . ."

"No," she said. "I'm paying and I'm entitled to watch the entertainment that *I* like."

"I suppose," said Grimes, "that it is an acceptable substitute for the real thing."

She turned away from the playmaster to look at him. Her eyes, magnified by black-rimmed spectacles that she wore, seemed enormous. Her wide, scarlet mouth distracted his attention from her sharp nose. Viewed through an alcoholic haze she was beginning to look definitely attractive.

She said, "I thought you'd never get around to it. Here I've been, cooped up in this flying sardine can, with an allegedly virile, rough and tough spaceman, and nothing, but nothing, has happened to me. Yet." She grinned. "My bunk or yours?"

"Mine," said Grimes.

She unfolded herself from her chair, all two metres of her. She touched the sealseams at the shoulders of her gown. It fell around her feet. Under it she was wearing nothing. As so often is the case with slender women her figure looked much fuller when she was naked than when clothed. Grimes got out of his shorts and shirt with fumbling haste. By the time that he was stripped she was already stretched out on his bunk on the starboard side of the cabin. He joined her.

And at the touch of her flesh all his desire faded.

She pushed him off her and he fell to the deck.

She got off the bunk and stood over him, sneering.

"A big, tough spaceman! And just because those obscene animals you carried in this ship on your last voyage tried to castrate you you're acting like a pussy-panicked pansy!"

She knew about *that*, thought Grimes. His killing of the beasts, valuable cargo, had landed him in a fine mess of financial and legal problems, had led to his being grounded on Bronsonia and his accepting the job of shipkeeping aboard *Bronson Star*. But she didn't know of his traumatic experiences aboard the skyjacked freighter on her return voyage. That was his secret, his alone, and always would be.

She snarled wordlessly, went back to her chair, resumed her interrupted viewing of the pornographic programme. She did not bother to dress. Her hand, Grimes noticed, was resting on her lap, her fingers moving. But if she did not wish privacy he most certainly did.

He got unsteadily to his feet, arranged the folding screens that would shut off his bunk and a little space around it from the rest of the cabin.

Then he tried, miserably, to sleep.

Two

———◆◉◆———

Little Sister came to New Venusberg.

Grimes had heard, of course, of the fabulous pleasure planet but this was his first time there. Oddly enough it was also Fenella Pruin's first time on this world. The General Manager of Bronson Star Enterprises, however, had spent a few days on New Venusberg as part of a Trans-Galactic Clippers cruise. Although on holiday he had kept his eyes skinned and his ears flapping. He had gained the impression that there was something unsavoury—something even more unsavoury than was to be expected in a holiday resort of this nature—going on. He had decided that an investigation might well pay off and that Fenella Pruin would be ideally qualified to make it. She was known, of course, by her name and the likenesses of her that accompanied her syndicated material but it was unlikely that anybody would penetrate her disguise or her cover story. To the Venusbergers she would be no more—and no less—than a fortuitously rich bitch, ripe for the plucking.

Little Sister came to New Venusberg.

Grimes was not sorry that the voyage was over. Neither, she told him, was she. She sat with him in the control cab as he eased the pinnace down to Port Aphrodite. Among her many other faults she was a back seat driver. She took him to task for evincing interest in the chalk giantess that, viewed from the air, was a huge advertisement for the major entertainment for sale on New Venusberg. Cut out from the green turf she was, although the two white hillocks that were her breasts, the oval blue ponds that were her eyes must have been artificial. There was golden hair on the head and above the jointure of the thighs (a flowering creeper, Grimes later discovered) and her nipples (marked by a sort of lichen) were pink.

"If you were as interested in me as you seem to be in that thing," said Ms Pruin, "you might be some use."

"I'm getting my bearings," said Grimes.

9

"If you can't see the spaceport apron and the marker beacons from here," she said, "you should have your eyes examined. Come to that, you've other organs that need attention."

Grimes made a major production of filling and lighting his pipe.

"Must you smoke that vile thing, stinking the ship out?"

Since she herself smoked thin, black cheroots that had the cloying scent of cheap incense Grimes considered her censure unjustified and said so. A snarling match ensued, terminated by a voice from Port Aphrodite Aerospace Control.

"Control to *Little Sister*. May I remind you that your berth is marked by the three scarlet flashers? It is not, repeat not, between the White Lady's legs." There was a tolerant chuckle from the speaker of the NST transceiver. "Of course, Captain, I realise that you're in a hurry, but even so . . .''

"*Little Sister* to Control," said Grimes. "Just admiring your scenery."

"You'll find much more to admire once you're down," Control told him.

"And if you can do any more than just admire it," whispered Fenella Pruin viciously, "I, for one, shall be surprised."

"Shut up!" almost shouted Grimes.

"*What* was that, *Little Sister*?" demanded Aerospace Control.

"I was just talking to my passenger," said Grimes.

He applied lateral thrust, bringing the golden pinnace directly over the triangle of beacons, vividly bright in spite of the brilliance of the morning sun. He wondered, not for the first time, why Port Captains love to berth incoming vessels in a cramped huddle when there are hectares of spaceport apron vacant. But there was no ground level wind and *Little Sister* would fit in easily between what looked like one of the bigger TG Clippers and what was obviously a Shaara vessel; they were the only spacefaring people whose ships were almost featureless cones with a domed top.

Fenella Pruin asked, "Shaara? *Here*?"

"Why not?"

"But they're arthropods."

"And they have their vices. Almost human ones. Alcoholism. Gambling. Voyeurism . . ."

"You'd know, of course."

Grimes did know. Not so long before he and his then passenger, the attractive Tamara Haverstock, had been captured by a Shaara Rogue Queen, held prisoner, in humiliating circumstances, aboard the arthropod's ship.

All he said, however, was, "Let me get on with the piloting, will you?"

Little Sister fell slowly, but not too slowly. Grimes dropped her neatly between the two towering hulks. (He could have come down almost to ground level well clear of them and then made a lateral final approach but he couldn't resist showing off.) He saw duty officers watching from control room viewports, waved to them nonchalantly.

The underskids kissed the concrete.

The inertial drive—a clangorous cacophony to those outside but reduced by sonic insulation to a mere, irritable grumble inside the hull—fell silent as Grimes switched it off.

"We're here," he said unnecessarily.

"Do you expect me to give you a medal?" she asked.

The port officials came out to *Little Sister*, riding in a large, purple, gold-trimmed ground car. Normally junior officers of the departments concerned would have completed the clearing inwards formalities—initiated by Carlotti deep space radio fourteen days prior to arrival—but although space yachts were not uncommon visitors to New Venusberg golden ones most certainly were. What she lacked in size *Little Sister* made up for in intrinsic value.

So there was the Chief Collector of Customs in person, accompanied by two micro-skirted, transparently shirted junior customs officers. There was the Port Doctor; there was no need for him actually to sight the clean Bill of Health from Bronsonia—a formality usually carried out by Customs—but Grimes was being given VIP treatment. There was the Port Captain—and his visit was purely social.

Grimes produced refreshments. (The last batch of Scotch that he had cajoled out of the autochef would almost have passed for the real thing and as he had decanted it into bottles with genuine labels he did not think that anybody would know the difference.) He, Prunella Fenn (he must remember always to call her that) and the three men sat around one table in the main cabin while the two Customs girls went through the ship's papers at another.

The Port Captain divided his attention between the ersatz Scotch and Grimes' passenger. He was a big, florid man with a cockatoo crest of white hair, with protuberant, slightly bloodshot (to begin with) blue eyes, a ruddy, bulbous nose and a paunch that his elaborately goldbraided white uniform could not minimise. He looked more like the doorman of a brothel than a spaceman, thought Grimes. (But the Port Captain on a world such as Venusberg was little more than the doorman of a brothel.)

The Port Doctor—even though he, too, was dressed in gold-trimmed white—looked like an undertaker. He did not divide his attention but was interested only in the whisky. He picked up the bottle, studied the label, put it down again. He lifted his glass, sipped, raised his heavy black eyebrows, then sipped again. He was the first person ready for a refill.

The Collector of Customs was interested most of all in the financial side of things. What was the actual value of *Little Sister*? What was the possibility of various solid gold fittings being stolen and sold ashore during her stay in Port Aphrodite? What security arrangements was Grimes implementing?

Unwisely Grimes said that he was prepared to use arms, if necessary, to protect his property and was sternly told that the ship's laser and projectile pistols must be placed under Customs seal and that the two laser cannon—Shaara weapons that had been fitted while *Little Sister* was temporarily under the command of the Rogue Queen—must be dismantled.

But Grimes was not to worry, the Collector told him. A guard would be on duty at his ramp throughout. (Grimes did worry. He knew who would have to pay for that guard. According to the charter party the charterers would pay all *normal* port charges and the wages of an armed guard could be—almost certainly would be—argued not to be a normal port charge.)

Finally Prunella Fenn got a little unsteadily to her feet.

"I'm off," she announced. "Jock's going to show me a good time . . ."

Jock? wondered Grimes.

The Port Captain levered himself upright, his hands on the table.

"I'm ready, Prue, soon as you are."

"I'm ready, Jock."

As they left the cabin he already had his arm about her slender waist, his meaty hand on her hip.

The Port Doctor raised his thick eyebrows. The Collector of Customs grinned.

"Well, Captain," he said, "I'd best be off myself. Ingrid and Yuri will put your pistols under seal. As for your cannon—as long as you remove the crystals and put them in bond with the hand guns that will be sufficient. I'll arrange for the Customs guard.'' He grinned again. "And enjoy your stay. The only thing that's not tolerated here is gunplay.''

He left the cabin far more steadily than the Port Captain had done although he had imbibed at least as much.

Grimes excused himself to the doctor, went out of the ship. Using the recessed rungs in the shell plating he clambered up to where the cannon were mounted above the control cab. He removed the crystals. Back inside the hull he handed these to the two Customs girls, who put them into the locker allocated for the purpose together with the pistols. They sealed the door with an adhesive wafer, told him that although it looked flimsy it was not and could be removed only with a special tool.

They accepted a drink—after all, thought Grimes, they had earned theirs, they had been doing all the work—and then left.

"Have ye any more o' that quite tolerable whisky, Captain?'' asked the Port Doctor.

Three

—————•◉•—————

"That lass o' yours made a big hit with Jock . . ." said the doctor.

"She's no lass of mine," said Grimes.

"Just the two o' ye in a wee ship like this? An' it's not as though she's unattractive . . ."

"You don't know her," said Grimes, "like I do."

"She's no' one o' the Sisterhood, is she? She didn't impress me as being that way. But a rich bitch . . . She must be a rich bitch to charter a ship to run her about the galaxy. An' a rich bitch is what Jock's been a-huntin' for these many years. We were shipmates in the Waverley Royal Mail, in their passenger ships, before we came out to this sink of iniquity. He was rich-bitch-chasing then—although, to give him credit, he'd prefer one not so rich but with a modicum of looks to one with all the money in the universe but a face like the arse of a Wongril ape an' a figure like a haggis. He was too picky an' choosey. That was his downfall. But that's aye the way in passenger ships; it's no' the ones ye oblige that make the trouble but the ones ye don't . . .

"Still, it's the bawbies that Jock's after more than hot pussy. An' although there's no shortage o' hot pussy on New Venusberg the best of it has no bawbies attached. But ye mean to tell me that ye weren't interested in Prunella's bawbies?" He drained his glass, held it out for a refill. "Ah, but ye wouldn't be, would ye? A man who owns a solid gold spaceship, e'en though she's only a wee boat, 'll not be short of a bawbie."

"She's not a wee boat," said Grimes stiffly. "She's a pinnace. A deep-space-going pinnace. And she happens to be built of an isotope of gold only because her original owner, the Baroness d'Estang, liked it that way."

"An' ye bought her from yon Baroness? Then ye're no' sae badly fixed yerself."

The thickness of the doctor's Waverley accent, Grimes

14

decided, was in direct ratio to the amount of whisky imbibed. The more Scotch that went in the more that came out.

He said, ''I didn't buy her. She was a sort of parting gift. In lieu of back and separation pay.''

''An' ye let a woman like that slip through yer fingers? Still, I suppose she was ugly as sin an' old enough to be Methuselah's granny.''.

''She was neither. She just happened to prefer a villainous bastard called Drongo Kane to me.''

''Kane? Ye ken Drongo Kane? We hae dealings wi' the mon, though he's no' been here himself for a while. There's a wee laddy called Aloysius Dreeble, skipper o' *Willy Willy*, who comes the no'. She's owned by Able Enterprises. Get it? Kane . . . Able . . . Och, whatever ye say about Kane ye must admit that the mon has a fine, pawky wit.''

''Mphm.''

''But *Willy Willy* . . . An odd name for a ship . . . Would ye ken if he has a girlfriend called Wilhelmina or some such?''

''Willy Willy,'' said Grimes, ''is the Australian name for a small, local whirlwind. But what cargo does this *Willy Willy* bring here?''

''Passengers most o' the while.''

''So Kane's in the tourist racket now.''

''Whyfor should *ye* be sneering? Ye're in the tourist racket yerself, cartin' rich bitches hither an' yon atween the stars. An' talkin' o' rich bitches—just how rich is *your* rich bitch?''

Grimes remembered that he was bound by the charter party to give the charterer's representative all possible support. Now would be as good a time as any, he thought, to run her cover story up to the masthead and see if anybody saluted. He would show this drunken quack the specially printed issues of *The Bronson Star*. No doubt the Port doctor would pass the fictitious information on to his crony, the Port Captain. Then soon it would be common knowledge all over New Venusberg.

He got a little unsteadily to his feet.

''I've some newspapers here,'' he said. *''She* doesn't know that I've got them. They're rather amusing reading . . . A fascinating transition story . . . Miss Goody Goody into Good Time Girl?''

He got the papers out of a filing cabinet, made room on the table to spread them out, indicated the relevant paragraphs with his forefinger. The Port Doctor was not too drunk to read. He chuckled.

"Ah, weel, a big prize . . . An' so long as she stays clear o' the gamblin' she'll have a few credits left when ye lift off from here. O' course, she may be payin' for the services o' the local studs, an' they don't come cheap. She'll no' be gettin' much in the way o' service from Jock—I'm his doctor an' I should know . . ." He looked up, blinking, at Grimes. "An' are ye sure, Captain, that ye weren't obligin' her? For love or money?"

Grimes made a major production of not replying.

The Port Doctor laughed. "So ye're an officer an' a gentleman an' ye're no' tellin'." He added, far too shrewdly for Grimes' comfort, "Perhaps the way it was ye'd rather not." He poured the last of the bottle into his glass. "An' now, would ye be havin' soberups in yer medicine chest? Ye can prescribe for the both of us an' then I'll take ye tae see the sights."

The soberup capsules worked as advertised.

Grimes changed into informal civilian clothing. The evening might turn out to be a wild one and if he were going to make a public spectacle of himself he would prefer not to do so in uniform. The Port Doctor, it seemed, was not troubled by such scruples; he did not, as Grimes expected that he would, go first to his office for a change of attire.

The two men passed through *Little Sister*'s airlock. It was evening already. (Where had the day gone?) Outside the pinnace the air was warm, redolent with a heavy scent that might have been that of flowers but which Grimes suspected was artificial. The spaceport lights—except around an Epsilon Class freighter where cargo discharge was in progress—were of low intensity. The floodlights of the passenger liners had been turned on but at no more than a fraction of their normal power so that the big ships had the similitude of faintly luminous, shimmering, insubstantial towers. Music was coming from concealed speakers, drifting on the lazy breeze, a melodious throbbing and wailing of guitars. Romance, with a capital R, was in the air. It was as meretricious as all hell.

"Sing me a song of the islands . . ." muttered Grimes sardonically.

"What?"

"This atmosphere . . . So phonily Hawaiian . . ."

The doctor laughed. "I see what you mean. Or hear what you mean. I'd prefer the pipes meself."

"Mphm?"

They walked slowly across the apron to the entrance of the spaceport subway station, an orifice in the side of a single storeyed building the curves of which were more than merely suggestive, that did more than hint at open thighs. And as for the doorway itself. . . . Only on a world like this, thought Grimes, could one find such an architectural perversion. *Labia majora . . . Labia minora . . .* Even an overhanging clitoris . . . A dark, ferny growth to simulate pubic hair . . .

"Doesn't this make you feel like a pygmy gynaecologist?" asked Grimes as they passed throgh the pornographic portal, stepped on to the downward moving stairway.

"I got a nice fee for helping to design it," said the doctor.

Grimes looked with interest at the advertisements on either side of the escalator, each one of them a window on to various aspects of this world, each one of them a colourful, three-dimensional moving picture. WINE & DINE AT ASTARTE'S KITCHEN—EVERY DISH A PROVEN APHRODISIAC . . . And with partners like that at the dinner table, thought Grimes, what need for artificial stimuli? (But perhaps in his case there was. The psychic trauma sustained aboard *Bronson Star* and aboard *Little Sister* herself had yet to heal.) GIRLS! GIRLS! GIRLS! AT KATY'S KATHOUSE! Katy's Kathouse? Cats . . . Some of those wenches so lavishly displaying their charms looked like Morrowvians. That tied in. Drongo Kane had trade connections with this world and, quite possibly, had been recruiting on Morrowvia before he finally blotted his copybook on the planet of the cat people. But some of the other women . . . The escalator carried him on down before he could have a proper look. CAVALIER ESCORT SERVICE . . . This, obviously, was aimed at the female tourists. The escorts were tall, virile young men, impeccably clad in archaic formal finery, the fronts of their tight trousers suggestively bulging. Another display—IF YOU'RE TIRED OF ALL THE OTHER LADIES HAVE A WHIRL WITH LADY LUCK! After many a century the roulette wheel was still the universally recognised symbol for games of chance.

"Lady Luck," said the doctor. "That's where we're going."

"You're the doctor," said Grimes. (He did not care much for gambling but, for the time being, the sort of games that were much more to his liking seemed to be out.) "But I was thinking that, for a start, I'd like a change from my own cooking."

"Not to worry, Captain. Lady Luck feeds her patrons at no extra charge; she makes her profits on the tables and machines. Mind you, she's not made much out of me. Over a year I usually show a small profit myself."

They were on the station platform now, looking at the animated holograms adorning the walls. They were joined by three men, obviously spacers, officers from one of the ships in port. They knew the doctor, engaged him in conversation. Grimes—details of the Outward Clearance of *Epsilon Puppis* were of no great interest to him—studied the advertisements. Just when he had come to the conclusion that when you have seen one explicit amatory exhibition you've seen them all a single bullet-shaped car slid silently in, came to a stop. Bullet-shaped? There was intentional phallic symbolism in its design.

"This is ours," said the doctor.

He and Grimes boarded the vehicle, leaving the others on the platform. They were probably bound for the Kathouse or some similar establishment, thought Grimes, not without a twinge of envy.

As soon as the passengers were seated the car started off.

No matter what it looked like its motion was that of a bullet.

Four

━━━━◆◆◆◆━━━━

Lady Luck was only two stops from Port Aphrodite.

Again there was an escalator ride, this time up to ground level. Again there was the display of explicit advertising, holograms that Grimes had already seen and one or two new ones. He was intrigued by the advertisement for the Church of the Ultimate Experience. What did it have to offer? A Black Mass? Through the swirling, coruscating mists that filled the frame he could just see, or thought that he could see, what looked like a naked woman spreadeagled on an altar with an inverted crucifix in the background.

He and the doctor stepped off the moving staircase into a brightly lit foyer. There were mobiles composed of huge, luminous dice cubes suspended from the shallow dome of the ceiling. There were almost garish murals depicting court cards not only from Terran packs but from those used by other races in the galaxy addicted to their own forms of gambling. Grimes saw the Golden Hive, analogous to the human card player's Ace, and the Queen Mother, and the Princess, and the Drone, and the Worker-Technician. So the Shaara frequented this establishment. Gambling was one vice that they held in common with Man.

"When you've finished admiring the Art Gallery, Captain," said the Port Doctor, "we'll go in. There's a small charge at the door. Did you bring any money with you?"

"Yes," said Grimes. "I suppose that they'll take Federation credits . . ."

"They'll take anything as long as it's legal tender on its planet of origin. I'm not being mean, you understand, in asking you to pay us in. It's just that I've always found that if somebody else treats me it always starts my winning streak for the night."

"Mphm. But what about me?"

"For you there's beginner's luck."

"Mphm." Grimes was unconvinced but allowed himself to be led to the tall blonde standing at the door. She was the first

19

decorously clad female he had seen since landing at Port
Aphrodite. It made a change. (There was no change from the
Cr50 bill that he tendered.) She was severely attired in an
ankle length black skirt, in a long-sleeved, high-collared white
blouse with a black string tie. There was a black bow in her
hair. She smiled with professional warmth and wished the two
men luck.

"What first?" asked the doctor. "Two up? That's your
national game, isn't it?"

"Tucker," said Grimes.

"Tucker? What sort of game is that?" Comprehension
dawned. "Oh, it's *food* you mean. But we didn't come here
to eat."

"I did," said Grimes. He thought, *I may as well try to get
my fifty credits worth.*

"Oh, all right. This way."

The doctor led Grimes through the huge room, past the
roulette tables with the croupiers in their archaic black and
white uniforms and the players dressed in everything from
stiffly formal to wildly informal attire, pausing only to stop a
robot servitor trundling by with a tray of drinks. He took a
whisky for himself, sipped and remarked condescendingly,
"Not as good as yours, Captain." Grimes helped himself to
gin.

They continued through a smaller but still large chamber in
which the Two Up school was in progress. Grimes wondered
what coins were being used; they looked to be the same size
as antique Australian pennies. He was tempted to linger but
one effect that soberup capsules always had on him was to
stimulate his appetite. There were card rooms and others for
dice, and others in which brightly coloured sparks chased
each other around enormous screens. Most, although not all,
of the gamblers were human.

At last they came to the buffet. There were long tables
loaded with the kind of food that looks like advertisements for
itself, that sometimes—but not always—tastes as good as it
looks. There was a towering drinks dispenser with a control
panel that would not have looked out of place on the bridge of
a Nova Class battlewagon.

The doctor made straight for this and, with the ease of
long practice, pushed the buttons for a treble whisky. Grimes
picked up a plate and browsed. Was that caviare? It was. It
probably had not come all the way from the Caspian Sea on
Earth—from Atlantia? or New Maine?—but it was edible.

And those things like thin, pallid worms weren't at all bad
. . . And neither was the pork fruit salad, although this was at
its best only on Caribbea, the world to which that strange
organism, neither animal nor vegetable, was native.

Munching happily, he watched a tall, slim Shaara princess
indulging her taste for alcoholic sweetmeats. He had seen a
party of Shaara at one of the roulette tables, doubtless she
was of their number. He had always rather liked the bee
people, still did—with reservations. (He would never forget
what he had suffered at the hands—claws? talons?—of that
Rogue Queen.) He said to her affably, ''They don't starve us
here, Highness.''

She turned to look at him with her huge, faceted eyes. The
voice that came from the jewelled box strapped to her thorax
was a pleasant soprano.

''Indeed they do not, sir. And no matter what my Queen
Captain may say or do, I believe in getting value for my
money.''

Her Queen Captain . . . So she must be one of the officers
from the Shaara ship in port.

''Are you on a cruise?'' Grimes asked.

''Yes.'' If she had been endowed with a mouth instead of
mandibles she would have smiled. ''The ship is a hive with
more queens than workers. And are you a spaceman, sir? You
have the appearance.''

''Yes, Highness. I am master of the little ship berthed
between you and the TG wagon.''

Her eyes glared at him like multiple lasers. ''So your ship
is *Little Sister*. So you are the man Grimes.''

What had he said wrong?

''You are Grimes. My hive sisters were the Queen Captain
and her officers in the ship *Baroom*. We have heard only
rumours of what happened but we believe that you destroyed
that vessel.''

*After what they did to Tamara and myself, and to lots of
other people*, though Grimes, *they had it coming to them*.

But he said nothing and she said nothing more. They stood
there, glaring at each other, astronauts both, with much in
common professionally but culturally a universe apart. (But
was there such a difference? Terran adventurers, both before
and after the dawn of the Space Age, have behaved as
reprehensibly as did that Rogue Queen.)

The princess turned her back to him and walked stiffly
away, her iridescent wings quivering with rage.

Grimes moved on, in the other direction. The acrimonious encounter had spoiled his appetite. He wandered through a door other than the one by which he had entered, found himself in a room full of game machines.

He had always liked such contraptions.

He liked to match wits with computers in simulated space battles but he looked in vain for such entertainment here. The names shining—some softly, some garishly—above the glowing screens made it obvious that the devices had been manufactured for use on New Venusberg, possibly had been made on the pleasure planet. LOVE MARATHON . . . WHIP THE LADY . . . CHAIN ME TIGHT . . . And in the screens themselves, although none of the machines was fully activated, there were hints of pale, sinuously writhing limbs, of rounded breasts and buttocks.

CHASE ME AND . . .

The broadly hinting label appealed to Grimes. To play the game, he discovered, would cost him only a single one credit coin. He went to a change maker, inserted a twenty credit bill into the slot. Silver coins rattled into the receptacle. But they were not coins, only tokens, each bearing on both sides Lady Luck's stylised roulette wheel. Presumably they could be spent only in this establishment.

Grimes pocketed all the metal discs but one, went back to the machine of his choice. There were no manual controls. There was a sort of padded hood into which he was to insert his head with eyepieces that looked into a replica of the overhead screen. This depicted only what looked like the back view of a naked woman regarded through a heavy mist. He withdrew, located the coin slot, inserted the token then put his head back into the hood.

The screen came alive.

There was a naked woman—slender, but not too much so—with her back to him. She was standing in a forest glade, her pale skin in vivid contrast to the dark foliage of trees and bushes. Grimes was naked too; he could feel the air cool on his skin, the grass damp under his feet. Suddenly this female whose face he had yet to see became the most desirable object in all the universe. He would creep up on her, throw her to the ground and . . .

He must have made some slight, betraying noise.

She turned her head, looked back at him over her smooth

shoulder. Her face, framed by long, golden hair, was more
than merely pretty, her eyes a wide, startled blue, her mouth
a wide, scarlet gash. Her expression combined fear and
invitation.

She ran.

Grimes ran.

She was fast and Grimes, he realised, was badly out of
condition. But those creamy buttocks, those long thighs,
fantastically beautiful in motion, drew him like a powerful
magnet.

She ran.

Grimes ran.

He was gaining on her.

He would catch her when she blundered into that bush with
the great, purple blossoms.

At the very last moment she changed direction, veering
sharply to the right. Grimes was not able to check himself.
The shrub, as well as blossoms, bore very sharp thorns.

He extricated himself, cursing. He could feel the blood
trickling down his lacerated skin. And she was standing there,
legs apart, hands on hips, laughing.

There was only one thing to do to her . . .

But she evaded his clutching hands as she turned, running
again, flitting between the trees like a pale wraith. He was
after her, losing ground at first then gaining until he stumbled
over a tree root; the pain in his bare foot was excruciating.
She paused then, looking back, laughing again. Her teeth
were very white against the scarlet of her lips.

She let him almost reach her, then was off again.

And they were out of the wood.

Ahead there was a low hill and on its summit there was a
building—a temple? White, it was, with pillars, bright against
the somehow ominous dark blue sky. Grimes *knew* that he
must catch her before she reached this sanctuary.

He would have done so had it not been for the swamp
between hill and forest. She knew the path across it, leaping
gracefully from grassy hummock to grassy hummock. He did
not. He was knee-deep, thigh-deep in stinking ooze before he
realised that he must keep to those patches of longer, darker
grass, as she was doing.

But she wanted to be caught.

She waited for him on solid ground, laughing still, legs
wide-spread, small, pink-nippled breasts provocative.

She waited for him until he had almost gained solidity then

turned again, running up the hill. Grimes pursued, his heart thudding, his lungs pumping. He actually got a hold on the long, golden hair floating behind her—and it came away in his hand. Beneath the wig was golden hair again, but short.

She vanished into the colonnade.

Stupidly Grimes stood there.

Should he follow?

Should he withdraw his head from the hood?

Later he wished that he had done so at this juncture.

They boiled out of the temple, the women, vicious, naked, sharp in tooth and claw. Jane Pentecost he recognised, and the Princess Marlene. There were Una Freeman and Maya, Mavis and Maggie Lazenby. And Michelle d'Estang and fat Susie. And the obnoxious Fenella Pruin as she had been when she derided him after his failure, and Tamara Haverstock . . .

He turned, pounded down the hill.

He could hear them after him, their surprisingly heavy feet, their shrill, hateful screams. He reached the edge of the swamp. He made a leap to the first little hummock, landed on it, stood there teetering for long, long seconds before jumping for the next.

He missed it.

And they were on him.

Their sharp teeth, their long fingernails were tearing his skin and the flesh beneath it. Their discordant laughter was loud in his ears. There was screaming, too—and loudest of all was his own.

The screen went blank, but he remained crouching there, his forehead pressed into the padding of the hood. His clothing was soaked in perspiration—and worse.

The screen went blank—but the hateful female laughter persisted.

Slowly he withdrew his head, looked around.

Fenella Pruin was there, the embarrassed looking Port Captain by her side. With a visible effort she stopped laughing.

"Grimes, Grimes . . . What an imagination you have! But do I *really* look like that in your eyes? A sort of nudist Dracula's daughter?"

"You watched in the monitor screen . . ." half asked, half stated Grimes.

"Of course. It's what it's for, isn't it?"

"But you didn't see . . . me . . ."

"But we did, Grimes. We did—although you're far better looking and far better endowed in your perverted imagination than you are in actuality. And we saw what happened to you. Proper bloody it was, too." She turned to her escort. "Why don't you see if you can do any better, Jock? Go on, be a sport. I'll pay."

"No," said the Port Captain. *"No."*

"Goodnight," said Grimes.

Acutely and miserably aware of the state of his clothing he turned away from them, slunk through the gambling halls and down to the subway station. He did not have long to wait for a car back to Port Aphrodite.

The Customs guard at his airlock was far too cheerful.

"You look like you've had a fine night on the tiles, Captain!" he laughed.

"It was interesting," said Grimes shortly as he retreated into his own little sanctuary.

Five

![decorative divider]

He stripped off his soiled clothing, had a long, hot shower. Cleansed, he was beginning to feel better. And hungry. He went into the little galley and assembled a thick, multitiered sandwich, opened a can of cold beer. He carried these refreshments to his part of the main cabin, put them down on the deck by his bunk. He stretched out and then, his body disposed like that of an ancient Roman banqueter, munched and gulped. He almost finished the sandwich but was suddenly asleep before all the beer was gone.

He dreamed, re-enacting the game—but this time he caught the girl before she reached the temple. This time her hair did not come away in his hand. He turned her around, threw her to the ground, fell heavily upon her. His right knee prised her thighs apart. He . . .

The loud ringing of a bell jerked him back to reality.

Action Stations!

Then he realised where he was and that the noise was being made by somebody seeking admission to *Little Sister*. He got out of his bunk, reached for and shrugged into a light robe. The bell went on ringing, in short, irritable bursts.

He went aft to the airlock, operated the local controls. Prunella Fenn stood there, glaring at him. "You keep a tight ship," she snarled sardonically. "Are you afraid that the wild, wild women will come and get you?" She brushed past him, looked down at the remnants of his supper. "Didn't I hear somewhere that your Survey Service nickname was Gutsy Grimes?" She stooped to pick up the can of now-flat beer, sniffed it disdainfully. "I could do with a drink myself—but not this gnat's piss. Fix me one, will you? A large brandy on one, small rock."

"I wasn't expecting you back," said Grimes.

"Surely you weren't expecting me to spend all night with that fat, boring slob? But the drink, Grimes. Now."

He went to the galley, poured a generous measure of

brandy over one ice cube. She snatched it from him without thanks.

He said, "I'll rig the privacy screen."

"Don't bother," she told him. "I want to talk."

She gulped from her glass, put it down on the table and started to undress. There was nothing at all sensual about the display, not the merest hint of invitation. There were bruises, Grimes noted clinically, on the pale skin of her upper thighs. She saw what he was looking at, laughed shortly.

"There are times when a girl has to suffer to get a story. Or to get a lead . . ."

She picked up the glass again, sat down on her bed, facing him.

She said, "I think that I shall be able to blow the lid off two very unsavoury rackets. Soon I shall have the makings of a couple or three stories that will have readers and viewers all over the galaxy literally *drooling*. There's white slavery— that's been a sure seller for centuries. The others are even better . . ."

"*Better?*" echoed Grimes.

"You can bet your boots it is. Why do you think that the Shaara come here?"

"For the gambling?" hazarded Grimes.

"More than that. You told me yourself that the Shaara—or some of them—are voyeurs."

"Nothing especially sensational in that. You're a voyeur yourself. *You* watched what was happening to me in that damned machine."

"But that wasn't for real, was it? Anyhow, *you* should know what the Shaara are capable of. Didn't you and that postmistress wench have a rough time when you were prisoners of that Rogue Queen? The Shaara like to humiliate, torture even, other intelligent beings—but such practices are frowned upon on their own planets. *Here* they can indulge their vices. Money—enough money—can buy anything."

"I can't quite believe that even on New Venusberg human beings could make a profit from allowing their fellow men and women to be tortured."

"Grow up, Grimes! I've heard that you're something of an amateur historian—so you should know the extent of the evil of which humanity is capable. But you spacemen, for all your phoney machismo, lead very sheltered lives, know almost nothing about the *real* universe. There's a lot more to it than the clean, empty spaces between the stars!

"Anyhow, this commercialised sadism ties in with the white slave racket. Innocent little bitches—yes, and innocent little puppies—recruited on backward planets (and some not so backward) and brought here to make their fortunes (they think!) on fabulous Venusberg. An old friend of yours, Drongo Kane, is in the business up to his eyebrows . . ."

"That bastard!" growled Grimes.

"Jock told me that one of the ships Kane owns—*Willy Willy*—is due in shortly from a world called New Alice . . . I sort of gained the impression that he wasn't supposed to talk about it—but you know what men are like. When they're trying to make a girl they tend to boast, to show how big they are, how important. But there's only one way of being big that counts."

"Mphm."

"Where is New Alice? What sort of world is it?"

"I haven't a clue."

"You're the expert. Or supposed to be. You were hired as such."

"I still haven't a clue," growled Grimes. He got up from his bunk and padded to the playmaster, set the controls so that it was hooked up to the memory bank of the ship's computer. He hit the question mark symbol on the keyboard, then typed NEW ALICE.

The reply appeared in glowing letters in the screen: NO DATA.

Fenella Pruin laughed. "That thing is as useless as you are."

Grimes' prominent ears flushed angrily. He said, "This memory bank, especially insofar as navigational data is concerned, is as good as anything in a battleship."

"So *you* say." She yawned, not bothering to hide her gaping mouth with her hand. "Another drink, then I'll be ready for a spot of shut-eye. And don't *you* come mauling me. I've had enough of that for one night."

He refilled her glass. She downed its contents in one gulp; some of the amber spirit dribbled down her chin and on to her breasts. Grimes felt no desire to lick it off. She stretched out on her bunk, not bothering to cover herself. Grimes stretched out on his, operated the switch at its head that dimmed the cabin lights.

She went to sleep almost at once, snoring not unmusically.

He found it hard to get off again. Two names kept flashing

before his mind's eye like an advertising sign: DRONGO KANE. NEW ALICE.

He already knew far too much about Kane—but where the hell was New Alice?

Six

———◆———

Even after a late and disturbed night Grimes was inclined to
be an early riser. He did not always greet the dawn with a
song, however; this was such a non-choral occasion. He
ungummed his eyelids, looked up blearily at the golden
deckhead. He had omitted to close various doors before retiring and the morning sunlight was streaming through the
control cab viewports, was reflected from burnished metal.
He groaned softly. He slowly pushed the bed cover down
from his body, swung his feet to the deck. He looked across
to Fenella Pruin's bunk. She was still sleeping, her right
forearm covering her eyes and most of her face. The rest of
her was uncovered. If Grimes had been feeling stronger he
would have been sexually stirred by the sight of her naked
body, as it was he felt only disgust. In her sluttish posture,
with the dark bruises on the skin of her inner thighs, she
looked *used*. And used, moreover, by that fat slob of a Port
Captain.

He padded aft to the little galley, switched on the coffee
maker. After a second or so he was able to draw a steaming
mug of the dark fluid. He added sugar, stirred. He sipped
cautiously. He felt a little stronger. He allowed the coffee to
cool slightly, then gulped and swallowed.

"Must you make that disgusting noise at this jesusless
hour?"

He looked around. Fenella Pruin was sitting up in her bed,
glaring at him.

"And you might put something on," she added. "Your
hairy arse isn't the sort of sight that I like to wake up to."

Grimes muttered something about pots and kettles.

She ignored this. "And what's that you're drinking? Don't
you ever stop stuffing yourself?"

"Coffee."

"Why didn't you say so before? Well, you can bring me
some. With cream. And sugar. You know how I like it."

Grimes did know. More than once during the voyage from

30

Bronsonia he had wondered if he were owner-master or cabin steward; the Pruin had been determined to get her—or her employer's—money's worth. He made coffee to her requirements, brought it to her. As he handed her the mug he was strongly tempted to slop some of the scalding fluid over her uncovered breasts. She snatched it from him ungraciously and a few drops were spattered on to her stomach.

"You clumsy oaf!" she snarled.

He did not feel obliged to apologise. He left her mopping her belly with the bed cover and went to the minuscule bathroom. After he had showered and depilated and all the rest of it he walked back to his side of the main cabin, ignoring the way in which she glowered at him. He took a brightly patterned civilian shirt from its hanger in his locker, hesitated between a pair of orange shorts and a kilt in the astronauts' tartan, gold, blue and silver on black. He decided on the shorts; he was never really happy in a kilt.

"A sight for sore eyes," she remarked sourly. "You're making mine sore. Going some place?"

"Probably. Do you want breakfast?"

"Two four minute hen's eggs, with buttered toast. Orange juice. Coffee."

There was no *please*.

"We're out of fresh eggs but the autochef can do you scrambled eggs or an omelette."

"Why are we out of fresh eggs?"

"Because I haven't ordered any stores yet."

"Why not? In my girlish innocence I assumed that the service in a chartered spaceship would be slightly superior to that in an Epsilon Class tramp."

"If your friend the Port Captain and the others hadn't been underfoot all day yesterday . . ."

"If *you* hadn't made such a pig of yourself every breakfast time there'd have been some eggs left."

The bells rang. Somebody was outside the ship seeking admission.

"See who it is!" she snapped.

Grimes went to the airlock, opened both doors. The Port Captain was there. His face was still florid but it was an unhealthy looking flush. His gorgeous uniform looked sleazy. More than ever he looked like the doorman of a brothel rather than a spaceman.

"Morning," he grunted. "Miss Fenn on board?"

"Where else, Captain McKillick? But come aboard. This is

Liberty Hall, you can spit on the mat and call the cat a bastard.''

"You can't come aboard until I'm presentable," called Fenella Pruin.

"Miss Fenn's not dressed yet," said Grimes.

"That doesn't worry me," said the Port Captain, managing a faint leer. "I don't suppose that it worries you either."

"It doesn't," said Grimes.

"You can say that again!" came the voice from within *Little Sister*. "Whoever perpetuates that myth about big, strong, virile spacemen wouldn't know if a big black dog was up him!"

Grimes' prominent ears reddened. the Port Captain superimposed an angry flush on his normally ruddy complexion. (After all he was—or had been—a spaceman himself.)

But he said, "I like a woman with a little fire in her."

"Mphm," grunted Grimes.

"Last night for example . . ."

"Mphm?"

"Never kiss and tell, eh, Captain? I can take a hint. But that dance she did at the Kathouse put the professionals to shame. In fact Katie told her that she'd give her a job if she ever wanted one. It was the business with the bottle and the two wine glasses that really impressed her, though . . ."

Grimes active imagination treated him to a series of lubricious mind pictures.

"When you've quite finished gossiping like a couple of old women you can come in," called Fenella Pruin.

Not only had she made herself presentable but had actually tidied up the main cabin. Inflatable chairs were set around the collapsible table, on which stood the golden coffee pot and its accessories. She was wearing an ankle length dress of patterned spidersilk, grey on grey, under which it was obvious that she was naked. From the neck down there was nothing at all wrong with her.

"Good morning, Jock," she said with spurious sweetness. "Coffee?"

"Thank you, Prue."

"Breakfast?" asked Grimes, whose belly was rumbling.

"I've had mine. Such as it was."

"Well, I'm having mine. Miss Fenn?"

"You mentioned omelets earlier . . . Something savoury if your autochef can manage it."

Grimes went into the galley to initiate the process of cookery. He could overhear the conversation.

"Last night—or early this morning—I asked Captain Grimes about that world you told me about. New Alice. He didn't know a thing, of course. Nor did his computer."

The Port Captain laughed. "Hardly surprising. It's one of Drongo Kane's secrets. My guess is that it's a Lost Colony that he's keeping to himself."

"A fine, profitable source of slave labour. Or white slave labour."

"Not that, Prue. The girls are paid. They aren't *slaves*."

"But they are exploited. I noticed last night that they were in great demand. Of course some men would find those oddly shaped legs of theirs very attractive . . . Do you suppose that they're mutants? Like those wenches from Heffner with two pairs of breasts . . ."

"Just a stroll down mammary lane," said Grimes, bringing in the omelets.

"Ha," said Fenella Pruin. "Ha, bloody ha! I am rolling on the deck in paroxysms of uncontrolled mirth."

"Ha," growled Grimes. "Ha, bloody ha."

"Give me my breakfast and stop the bloody clowning."

"Actually," said the Port Captain, adopting the role of peacemaker, "it was rather neat. Mammary lane, I mean. Our genes or chromosomes or whatever—I'm only a spaceman, not a biologist—must hold the memories of all the stages of evolution through which we, as a race, have passed . . ."

"Thanks for the mammary," said Grimes.

"You get on my tits," snarled the Pruin.

"But these females with the odd legs," Grimes persisted, "what sort of hair do they have?"

"Just hair," the Port Captain told him. "Reddish brown mostly, in the usual places."

"Mphm." Grimes admitted that he had been adding two and two to make five. He had been more than half way to the assumption that there was no such world as New Alice, that Drongo Kane was recruiting on Morrowvia. But the description of the exotic wenches in Katy's Kathouse didn't fit. Morrowvian women were perfectly formed, although their hair was like a cat's fur and could be any of the feline colourations, even to tortoiseshell.

Meanwhile Fenella Pruin had wolfed her omelet. She got to

her feet, saying, "I'm ready for the road, Jock. Oh, Grimes, fix your front door so that it lets *me* in. I'm not sure what time I shall be back."

"I have to record your voice pattern."

"Then do it."

After she had spoken into the microphone she said to Grimes, "Why don't you have a look at Katy's Kathouse? You seemed interested enough."

Somehow it was more of an order than a suggestion. She was sniffing out something, something that stank, and he was appointed apprentice bloodhound.

Seven

It was too early in the day, he thought, to go cathouse crawling. Surely there must be some way of occupying the time on this planet during daylight hours. There was a pile of brochures on board, left by the boarding party; neither he nor Fenella Pruin had gotten around to studying these. He found them under her bunk. He leafed through them. Most of them advertised after-dark attractions but a few catered for those not sleeping off the previous night's debauchery.

New Bali Beach . . .?

It looked promising. His wardrobe did not include swimming trunks but, if the photographs of the seaside resort were to be believed, such attire would not be necessary. But money would be. Those waterside cafés, with beautiful, naked people sitting under gaily coloured umbrellas sipping their long drinks and nibbling their exotic foods, looked extremely expensive. Most of the advance monies given to him by *The Bronson Star* had gone to pay his outstanding debts on Bronsonia. Fenella Pruin had plenty of money with her— there was a huge wad of currency in *Little Sister*'s safe—but there would be a most distressing scene if he helped himself to a small loan. She would have to give him some sooner or later; if she wanted him to assist her in her muckraking she would have to pay his expenses. But he doubted if she would be willing to treat him to a day at the seaside.

He decided to take his lunch with him.

In the galley he constructed a pile of thick sandwiches; the ham that he had purchased back on Bronsonia wasn't at all bad and there was a cheese with character. He decanted chilled wine into an insulated flask. He put the food and the drink into a shoulder bag.

He decided to call the Port Doctor before leaving the ship, got through without trouble on *Little Sister*'s NST radio to the spaceport switchboard. An attractive redhead told him that Dr MacLaren was free and would take his call. Then MacLaren scowled at him from the little screen.

"Oh, it's *you*, Captain Grimes. Where the hell did you get to last night?"

"I couldn't find you, so I went back to the ship."

"You didn't look very hard. And I *needed* you, man. A combination of your beginner's luck and my system and we'd have cleaned up. As it was . . ."

"Mphm."

"Well, what can I do for you?"

"I was thinking of going out to New Bali for the day."

"I'm not stopping you."

"I thought that you might know something about the place."

"I went there once and didn't like it. Is that all?"

So the Good Doctor, thought Grimes, was blaming him for his previous night's losses. Subsidised by Grimes, he would be convinced, he would have been able to ride out the bad run and would have won a fortune on the ensuing good one. It was just too bad—but Grimes still had most of *his* money in his pocket.

"I'll be seeing you," said Grimes, terminating the conversation.

He left the ship, exchanged a few words with the bored Customs guard, then walked to the subway station. There were few signs of life about the spaceport. The liners, like huge, lazy beasts, were drowsing in the warm sunlight and somnolence would also be the order of the day inside the great, shining hulls. Grimes felt virtuous.

In bright daylight the entrance to the station looked very tawdry. That tawdriness was somehow passed on to the advertisements on either side of the escalator and on the platform. He found one that was not a depiction of fleshly delights but a map of the railway system. He discovered that he would have to take a Number 9 car.

He did not have long to wait for it. He was the only passenger. He reflected that there was one great advantage of public transport; nobody had to worry about whether or not it was making a profit. To pass the time on the journey he read the paper that he had obtained from the automatic dispenser, a neatly folded packet of news sheets. It should have been free; there were far more advertisements than news items.

Spacemanlike, he turned first to the shipping information. He noted that *Little Sister*, Captain John Grimes, Far Traveller Couriers, with passengers, was in port. *Passengers?* He supposed that "passenger" would have looked rather absurd. And *Broorooroo*, Queen-Captain Shrim, Shaara Interstellar

Transport, was in. And *Taiping*, Trans-Galactic Clippers,
Captain Pavel. And . . .

But who was due?

Delta Geminorum, Captain Yamamoto, Interstellar Transport Commission, passengers and general cargo. *Empress of
Scotia*, Captain Sir Hector Macdonald, Waverley Royal Mail,
cruise. *Rim Wyvern*, Captain Engels, Rim Runners, bulk
fluids.

And *Willy Willy*, Captain Dreeble, Able Enterprises,
passengers.

So . . .

He turned to the social columns.

He learned that the charming Miss Prunella Fenn, of
Bronsonia, was being escorted around the night spots by Port
Captain Jock McKillick and that Queen-Commissioner Thrum,
from Shreell, was still enjoying her holiday on New Venusberg.
The photograph of Fenella Pruin made her look almost beautiful.

There was a crossword puzzle. The answer to every clue
was either obscene or anatomical or both. Grimes, who was
fond of word games, was able to solve it without too much
mental strain. After all, that ancient Nilotic peasant with his
Spanish uncle engaged in non-productive intercourse was obvious enough . . .

The car arrived at his station. He disembarked. There was
the usual platform with the usual advertising, the usual escalator.

He emerged on to a wide promenade, paved with some
veined, polished stone. Landward were buildings, shops mainly,
few higher than one storey, their wide windows agleam with
the merchandise on display. Further inland was a tower—a
hotel?—that was a huge and unashamed phallic symbol. On
the other side of the wide walkway was the beach—dazzling
white sand, gaudy sun umbrellas, sprawling human and humanoid bodies ranging in colour from pink to the darkest
brown. It was all very nice but it was nothing like Bali as he
remembered that island, even though the trees that cast their
shade over the walk were not dissimilar to Terran palms.

He stood there for a few moments taking his bearings. He
watched a trio approaching him. There was a man, uglily
obese, with his skin burned to an ugly pink, naked save for
the straps of the cameras and recorders slung about his torso.
There were two girls, tall, slim brunettes, each clothed in
golden tan, with golden chains about their waists, with golden
anklets and bracelets, with jewels gleaming between their
breasts, in their navels and in their pubic hair. Before they

reached him they turned to look into the window of a jeweller's shop. They went inside. Grimes wondered how the tourist was going to pay for more ornaments for his mercenary girlfriends, came to the conclusion that one of those camera cases must really be a money pouch.

More naked pedestrians passed him. The outworlders were easy to spot, even though some of them, male and female, were quite well made. They, apart from their cameras and money pouches, were . . . naked. Although splendidly nude the local boys and girls were all dressed up like Christmas trees.

He walked across the promenade. Next to the wide steps down to the beach was one of those expensive looking cafés. There was a showcase outside with representations—wax or plastic?—of the various edibles and potables on sale, together with prices. Grimes congratulated himself on his foresight; having brought his lunch with him he would not have to beggar himself by paying a minor monarch's ransom for a ham sandwich. But he did hire a beach umbrella. The price he paid for a few hours' use of the thing could have purchased at least two similar articles on most worlds. He kicked off his sandals, picked them up and walked towards the sea. Some of the supine or prone ladies turned their heads to follow his progress but soon lost interest. Perhaps, he thought, there had been some mutation on New Venusberg resulting in X-ray vision so that these wenches could ascertain at a glance how much money was in his slim wallet . . .

A few metres from the water's edge he drove the ferrule of his umbrella into the sand then opened it. He stripped, enjoying the feel of the sunlight on his bare skin; as he always made daily use of *Little Sister*'s ultra violet lamp there would be no risk of sunburn. Putting his shoulder bag and clothing in the shade of the parasol he walked down to the sea. There was almost no wind and the incoming waves were mere ripples. He waded out until he was chest-deep and then let himself fall forward. He struck out with arms and legs, but lazily, making deliberately slow progress through the slightly too warm water. He turned so that he was swimming parallel to the shore so that he could keep an eye on his possessions. He did not think that there was any danger of theft but it would be rather embarrassing if he were obliged to return to his ship naked and penniless.

He began to feel thirsty.

He waded out from the sea, back to the bright umbrella. He

opened his bag, took out the insulated flask. The wine was delicious. He unwrapped a sandwich. That was good too. He noticed that people around him were looking at him disdainfully—the elegant, bejewelled girls who had already made assessment of his comparative poverty, the muscular, deeply tanned, well endowed young men. He heard them talking to the tourists whom they were with, the plump matrons and the pot-bellied males. He heard laughter that had a derisive edge to it.

Fuck 'em, he thought. There was no law that said that he must spend his hard-earned money on this clip joint of a planet. He wiped his mouth with the back of his hand and then, to compound the deliberate coarseness, the back of his hand on his right buttock. He stretched out on his back, using his bag for a pillow. After smoking a soothing pipe he surrendered himself to the drowsy warmth, slid into unconsciousness.

He was not asleep for long.

He was awakened by a steady droning noise coming from overhead. He opened his eyes, looked up. It was a party of Shaara flying over the beach, two princesses and three drones, their wings an iridescent blur in the sunlight. One of them swooped low, her huge-faceted eyes staring down at Grimes. Then the party veered inland, making a descent at the beachside café.

"Even *they* can afford to buy a drink," Grimes heard one of the girls in his vicinity say to her portly male companion. The tourist muttered in reply that spacebums should be confined to their ships.

Fuck 'em, thought Grimes again.

He was just dozing off when the Shaara came back over him. He woke up with an unplesant start when the soft containers that had held some sticky, sickly smelling confection, that were no more than three quarters empty, spattered down on to his naked body.

He scrambled to his feet, cursing. He would have thrown something at the retreating Shaara if they had not been already out of range. He glared around at the grinning faces of the other sunbathers. Then, with what dignity he could muster, he walked into the sea to wash off the slimy mess.

When he came out of the water a darkly tanned, heavily muscled young man, naked save for a white brassard with BP in black, carrying a shoulder bag, strode up to him. He pointed sternly to the scum on the surface of the water, the shreds of plastic, and demanded, "Did *you* do that?"

"I was bombed," said Grimes.

"Inebriation, no matter how induced is no excuse for pollution," said the beach patrolman.

"I was bombed, I'm telling you."

"I heard you the first time. The fine will be one hundred Federation credits, or the equivalent, if paid on the spot. Otherwise you will have to appear in court."

"But these people," argued Grimes, with a sweeping gesture of his arm, "can tell you . . ."

"He made a mess all over himself," said one of the girls, "and then went to wash it off in our clean sea."

"The Shaara . . ." insisted Grimes.

"Come off it, fellow. Whoever heard of one of *them* going into the water? But I haven't got all day to waste on you. Are you paying up—if you *can* pay—or are you coming with me to be charged?"

Grimes paid up.

Then he dressed and returned to *Little Sister*.

Eight

He spent the remaining daylight hours catching up with his housekeeping. He called the Port Aphrodite provedores and ordered a few items of consumable stores, including the fresh hen's eggs that his passenger had been pining for. These were delivered almost at once. When he signed the bill he wondered if those cackleberries came from the fabulous goose but they were neither large nor aureately shelled.

When everything had been stowed away he cleaned up, then dialled a simple but satisfying meal on the autochef—rare steak and onions with French fried potatoes, a hot, crisp roll with cheese and salad. Presumably refreshments would be available at Katy's Kathouse but he could not be sure if it would be free, or included in the price of admission. He suspected that it would be hellishly expensive—but if it did happen to be gratis he could always find room for a substantial supper.

He attired himself in semi-formal evening wear—ruffled white shirt, sharply creased black trousers, highly polished, calf-length black boots. Normally he did not much care for dressing up; his assumption of the modest finery was, perhaps, a reaction to the humiliation of the afternoon.

He let himself out of the ship, passed the time of day briefly with the Customs guard, walked slowly across the spaceport apron to the subway station. The evening was warm. The sky was dark and clear and in it floated an advertising balloon, spotlit from below, that was a quite explicit depiction of a naked woman. She was, thought Grimes, definitely pneumatic . . . In the soft lighting the station entrance was once again erotic rather than blatantly pornographic. It promised more, much more, than could ever be attained on a highly commercialised pleasure planet such as this.

Other pleasure seekers were abroad, proceeding in the same direction as himself—passengers from the cruise liners, spacemen and -women. He rode down on the escalator be-

41

hind a fat man and two plump, no-longer-young ladies. He
could not help overhearing their conversation.

"You really should have come out to the beach with us,
William. Laugh? I thought I'd die! There was this man, a
spacer. No, not from our ship, but a penny pincher all the
same. You know the type. Lording it aboard their tin cans in
their pretty uniforms and generous as hell with their entertainment allowance grog but too mean to spend a cent when they
get ashore. He'd actually brought his lunch with him. In a
bag! And then there he was, soaking up the sun—that was
free!—when these Shaara flew over. They zoomed in to that
rather nice eatery and ordered the sort of sweet, sticky muck
that they like. And then they collected up all the *soggy*
containers and took off and *bombed* the man. You should
have seen his face! And I thought that his big, flapping ears
were going to burst into flame . . ."

"People like that shouldn't go to places that they can't
afford," said the man. "Oh, well. It taught him a lesson."

"He was taught a lesson, all right. He went down to the
sea to wash himself off. Then the beach patrol came on the
scene and fined him on the spot for polluting the ocean.
When he pulled the money out of his wallet you'd have
thought he was bleeding to death . . ."

"*Spacemen*," sneered the male tourist. "They're all the
same. They spend practically all of their lives in their little,
artificial worlds and just don't know how to behave themselves on the surface of a decent planet."

They reached the bottom of the escalator. Grimes followed
the party of tourists on to the platform. The plump, improbable blonde, still chattering to her companions, turned to look
at the advertisements on the wall and came face to face with
the subject of her funny story. She froze in mid-sentence. She
blushed spectacularly—her face, her neck, her shoulders, the
overly full breasts that were revealed rather than concealed by
the translucency of her dress. Her small mouth, which had
been open, opened still wider.

Grimes looked at her coldly. He said politely, "I can set
your mind at rest, madam. I could well afford that fine. I am
the owner as well as the captain of *Little Sister*. You must
have noticed her . . ."

"The *golden* ship," she whispered.

"Yes. The golden ship. As I have said, I could afford the
fine. I just resented having to pay it in those circumstances."

(That last was true enough.)

He turned on his heel, walked away along the platform, his little triumph already turning sour. Was an eccentric billionaire—as that foolish, snobbish woman must now be regarding him—any better than a rough, poverty stricken spaceman?

The car came in. Grimes was one of the first to board. He noticed that the woman and her friends sat as far away from him as possible. He was among the first out at the Katy's Kathouse station. The plump blonde and the other two also disembarked but stayed well behind him.

The foyer of the Kathouse was at the head of the escalator. Grimes had been expecting something highly erotic but he was disappointed. Black-draped walls, a black ceiling . . . Faint, flickering light from tall, white candles . . . Vases of white flowers—natural? artificial?—that looked like lilies . . . A faint mumur of funereal organ music . . .

Was this the right place?

There was a pay booth by a black curtained doorway, manned by a cadaverous individual clad in rusty black with the merest hint of white at wrists and throat. Grimes approached this gentleman.

"Three hundred credits," croaked the doorkeeper.

"Does that include refreshments?" asked Grimes.

"Of course," he heard the plump lady whispering somewhere behind him, "the very rich are *mean* . . . That's how they get to be rich."

"Do you take us for a charitable institution?" the man asked rudely.

Grimes paid up, passed through the curtain.

Inside there was more darkness—but soft, rosy, caressing. A girl materialised before Grimes, her face and blonde hair pallidly luminous above her severe, chin, to ankle black dress.

"A table, sir? For one?" Her voice was pleasant, her accent Carinthian. "Please to follow."

The lighting flared briefly and rosily and she was naked before him. Yes, she was Carinthian all right. Face and body had the Siamese cat sleekness that was the rule rather than the exception among the women of Carinthia. The lights dimmed and she was fully clothed again. A good trick, thought Grimes. He wondered how it was done. Some special quality of the fabric from which her dress was made and something fancy in the way of radiation? He let her lead him between the tables. The lights flared again. Of those seated some were briefly nude and some were not—the professional companions, probably, and the customers.

She brought him to a small table for two, ignited the black candle in its white holder of convoluted plastic with a flick of a long fingernail. Grimes was amused by the symbolism; there was only one thing that the candle holder could possibly represent.

He sat down in the chair that she pulled out for him, looked at the menu and the wine list under the transparency of the table top.

"A drink, sir? Something to eat?"

It was just as well, he thought, that he had dined before coming ashore. Katy was not as generous as Lady Luck; probably her overheads were higher and her profits less certain. Twenty credits for a cheese sandwich—and that was one of the least expensive items. Twenty five credits for a small bottle of locally brewed beer . . .

"Just a beer," he said. "The Venuswasser."

"May I order for myself, sir? I am required to eat and drink with you."

At whose expense? wondered Grimes. It was a question to which the answer was obvious. *And champagne*, he thought. *And caviar.* But what did it matter? He would put the bite on his charterer for whatever he paid; after all she had as good as ordered him to come here. And if his immediate funds ran out he could always use his First Galactic Bank credit card.

The candle holder, he saw, was also a microphone. The girl spoke softly into the folds of the vaginal orifice. She ordered his beer first. She ordered champagne—imported, of course. (Grimes thought sourly that probably only the label on the bottle would be imported.) She ordered steak. She slipped several notches in Grimes' estimation; he always held that the only possible tipple with red meat was a red wine.

She smiled at him as the revealing lights flared up again. He was prepared to forgive her for her taste in wine. Her pink nippled breasts were just right, neither too small nor too large.

"May I have a cigarette?" she asked.

"I'm sorry. I don't use them."

She spoke again into the microphone, adding a pack of Virginia Slims to the original order—another imported and therefore expensive luxury.

Then she said, "Shouldn't we get better acquainted? I'm Tanya."

"Good to know you, Tanya. I'm John."

"You're a spacer, John, aren't you?"

"I have that misfortune."

She laughed prettily. "Stop kidding. I've known quite a few spacers. I prefer them to tourists. But they're all the same. They like women—but their real mistresses are their ships . . ."

"Mphm . . ."

A waitress appeared with the order. A black, half mask with attached pointed ears gave her a vaguely feline appearance; otherwise she was naked. Her figure was lumpy. She would have to do something about it if ever she were to graduate to hostess grade.

Tanya dismissed the girl curtly, cutting short her attempt to be pleasant to Grimes. She moved away ungracefully, resentment glowering from her bobbing buttocks. Grimes regretted being stuck with the Carinthian woman as his companion for the evening; all too obviously—at least insofar as her own sex was concerned—she was not one of those legendary whores with a heart of gold.

While he sipped his beer—it wasn't bad although it had a rather odd flavour—he watched her eat and drink. He thought: And they call *me* Gutsy! He listened to the sensuous throb of the music that came from the concealed speakers. He looked around at the other tables. To judge from the overloud laughter, the attempts to sing in time to the background melody, inhibitions were being shed. He felt like shedding a few himself. That beer was deceptively strong. Was alcohol the only intoxicant in its composition?

Rosy spotlights set in the ceiling came on, their beams directed on to the stage at one end of the big room, creating an ellipse of relatively bright illumination. The music was suddenly much louder. The tune was oddly familiar although at first he could not identify it. The tempo was subtly wrong, the rhythm distorted. Then he recognised it. Anger accompanied recognition. Although he prided himself of having shed his regional chauvinism long since he resented the misuse of that good old national song as a dancehall melody.

The girls pranced on to the stage. Pranced? No, he decided, that was not quite the right word. Hopped? Perhaps, perhaps . . . Yet that word was not adequate to describe the animal grace with which the women moved. They were small-breasted, their legs were heavily muscled. Their navels were abnormally deep. It was those lower thighs that interested Grimes most. (He had always been a leg man rather than a titman.) There

was something distinctly odd about the jointure—odd, but
somehow familiar.

A stout woman strode on to the stage when the music
stopped. Her ample breasts were almost spilling out of the
low cut black dress that was a second skin over her too ample
figure. Her face was chalky white under the flaming red hair,
her mouth small despite the great slash of lipstick that unsuc-
cessfully tried to create an illusion of generosity.

"Katy . . ." volunteered Tanya around a mouthful of steak.

"Who's for the kangaroo hunt?" bellowed Katy. "Pay yer
money at the door to the dressing room! Only a thousand
credits an' cheap at half the price! No extra charge for hire of
costumes!"

"Kangaroo hunt?" Grimes asked Tanya.

"One of the specialties of the house," she told him, with a
slight sneer. "Nature red in tooth and claw and all that." She
looked him over. "No. I don't think that *you'd* go for games
of that sort . . ."

But there was no shortage of volunteers. Men—tourists and
spacers—were getting up from their tables, walking to the
door to which Katy had gestured with her plump arm. They
paid their money to the girl at the cash desk, went inside. On
the stage the dancers were huddled together. They looked
frightened but there was more than fear on their faces.
Anticipation? Excitement?

There was music again—electronic yet disturbingly prime-
val and, to Grimes at least, evocative. He recognised the eery
whispering of didgerydoos, the rhythmic clicking of singing
sticks, the ominous, soughing bellow of bull roarers.

The first of the hunters came out from the dressing room.
He was naked and the skin of his body had been painted black
and that of his face in a ferocious design of white, red and
yellow. He was carrying a spear. Grimes stared; surely it was
not a real one. He was relieved to see that it was not. The
shaft terminated not in a blade but a ball.

One by one the other intrepid hunters emerged. A few
actually looked like real savages but most of them like what
they really were, fat, soft men in fancy undress. Some were
obviously embarrassed, a few were obviously eagerly looking
forward to the hunt.

A tourist woman yelled, "If you could only see yourself,
Wilberforce! I'll treasure this memory to my dying day!"

Katy called to her, "There'll be photographs on sale after

the hunt, dearie!'' Then, ''All right you great black hunters!
You've been told the rules! Go to it!''

The lights dimmed. The bodies of the naked women, still
on the stage, were faintly luminous as were the painted faces
of the hunters. The weird music continued and added to it
there was a distant howling, no doubt the idea of whoever
was playing the synthesiser as to what dingoes should sound
like. The girls were shuffling nervously, uttering little, animal
squeals.

A chill breeze blew through the vast room. Something
made Grimes look up towards the ceiling. It now had the
appearance of a black, clear sky with a scattering of bright
stars. Only one constellation was recognisable and that only
to Terrans—the Southern Cross.

The women were squealing more loudly now, jumping
from the stage. They were crouching as they hopped, their
hands held up to their breasts like forepaws. They scattered,
bounding between the tables. One of them brushed by Grimes.
Given a tail, he thought, she could have passed for a big,
albino kangaroo.

The hunted were familiar with the terrain, the hunters were
not. They blundered into tables, oversetting drinks. Some
were deliberately tripped by the outstretched legs of friends or
wives or mistresses. But the quarries would have to allow
themselves to be run down eventually. That was their job.
That was what they were being paid for.

The first 'kill'' was not far from where Grimes was sitting.
The huntsman, running with his spear extended before him,
just flicked his victim on the buttocks with the end of his
weapon. She screamed—and it was a real scream. She fell
face down, her body twitching.

The hunter yelled in triumph, pounced on to her, roughly
turned her over, spreading her legs. He coupled with her
brutally and briefly. He rolled off her, got unsteadily to his
feet. Grimes stared disgustedly into the man's face. Even
under the thick paint he thought that he could read shame. The
man muttered something, shambled slowly towards the dressing room.

Grimes looked down at the girl, sprawling supine on the
floor. She looked up at him. He was shocked by her expression,
by the hopelessness of it. He wanted to say something
comforting, to do something. He was half way out of his
chair when Tanya stopped him.

''Don't waste sympathy on the little bitch,'' she said harshly.

"She's making a damn sight better living here than she would be on her own lousy planet."

"And where is that?" asked Grimes.

"How should I know? There're girls here from all over the galaxy. None of us was pressganged."

"Mphm?"

"Of course not. Oh, I admit that getting back to Carinthia after I've made my pile won't be as easy as I thought it would be. Making my pile's the trouble. By the time I've paid the nominal—ha, ha!—rent for my room and bought a few rags and crusts there's not much left of my retaining fee. If it weren't for the generosity of tourists . . . And spacers . . ."

"Mphm."

"I'm being frank with you, John. If I take you up to my room I shall expect a present."

"I'm sorry," lied Grimes. "I have to be back aboard my ship soon. But if you can tell me anything about these girls there'll be a present for you."

"Cash on the nail," she said.

He went into a brief but intense session of mental arithmetic. There would be the bill for the meal and a tip for the waitress. Luckily he did not have to worry about paying his fare back to the spaceport. He extracted notes from his wallet, passed them to her.

"Is that all?" She shrugged. "Better than nothing, I suppose. Well, all I know about the big-bummed, flat-chested bitches is that they were brought here in Captain Dreeble's ship, the Willy Willy. They're under contract to Able Enterprises. Able Enterprises owns a big chunk of this Kathouse. Satisfied?"

"What language do they speak?"

"A sort of standard English. With an accent—rather like yours."

The lights were up again now. The last of the hunted girls had picked herself up from the floor and vanished from the room. The music was no longer eery but merely brassily strident. The stage was occupied by a giggling gaggle of tourist women, dancing lasciviously, tripping over the clothing that they were discarding. They were joined by a group of the hunters, still blackly and greasily naked.

Grimes waited for a while to see if anybody would be doing anything with a bottle and two wine glasses—but that must be, he decided, a party trick peculiar to Fenella Pruin. He asked Tanya to call for the bill. She did so. She scowled at him when he tipped the little waitress.

He said a not very warm goodnight to Tanya.

She said a not very warm goodnight to him.

There was no suggestion from either side that they should meet again.

He returned to his ship.

Nine

"And how did you find the Kathouse?" asked Fenella Pruin, regarding Grimes rather blearily over the breakfast table. Before he had time to reply she said, "These are bloody awful eggs. Where did you get them? Did you steal them out of a mud snake's nest?"

Grimes ignored this latter, answering only the first question.

"Expensive," he said. "You owe me . . ."

"*I* owe *you*? Come off it, buster!"

"I was helping you in your investigations . . ."

"You were having a bloody good time." She regarded him steadily, accorded him a derisive sneer. "Or were you? With your peculiar problem . . ."

"The fact remains," said Grimes, trying to ignore the burning of his ears, "that I had to pay my admission into the Kathouse. Then I was stuck with a bill for an expensive dinner . . ."

"For you and which floosie?"

"And then I purchased some information."

"Then spill it."

"What about my expenses?"

"You're a mercenary bastard, aren't you? All right. Let me have a detailed account, in writing, and I'll think about it. Get me some more coffee, will you? Then talk."

Grimes fetched more coffee.

He said, "In some ways the evening was disappointing. I didn't see anybody doing anything with a bottle and two wine glasses . . ."

She glared at him, snarled. "You don't have to believe everything that you hear—especially from that fat slob Jock McKillick! But did you see the specialty of the house, the kangaroo hunt?"

"Yes."

"Kangaroos are Australian animals, aren't they? You're an Australian. Was the hunt authentic?"

"Kangaroos aren't hunted. They're protected fauna."

"But they must have been hunted once. Centuries ago."

"I wasn't around then. Oh, all right, all right. I suppose that the hunt was an attempt to reconstruct a very ancient, long since dead nomadic culture. Of course, if I'd been stage managing it I'd have given the hunters woomeras and boomerangs . . ."

"What's a woomera? Some sort of weapon, I suppose."

"A spear thrower."

She laughed. "I can just imagine it. Lethal missiles mowing down Katy's customers . . ."

"It would be newsworthy," said Grimes. "Well, anyhow there was the weird music. As far as I know the Australian aboriginals didn't hunt to music—but those sounds did contribute to the atmosphere. The most convincing part of the hunt was the kangaroos themselves. Those girls with their odd legs . . . And it seems quite definite that they come from a world called New Alice and that they're brought here in Drongo Kane's ship, *Willy Willy*. The master is Aloysius Dreeble, who used to be Kane's mate in *Southerly Buster*."

"And they come from New Alice. Anything Australian about that name?"

"Yes. Alice Springs is a city in Central Australia. It's referred to usually just as Alice or the Alice."

"And not for the first time—where the hell *is* New Alice? Nobody seems to know. Not even you."

"One person will know," said Grimes. "Captain Aloysius Dreeble. And his ship is due in very shortly."

"How do you know?"

"I read the papers," said Grimes smugly.

Ten

———◆———

Willy Willy was not coming into Port Aphrodite. There was another spaceport on New Venusberg used only by vessels bring cargoes of an objectionable nature, the bulkies and others. Presumably *Willy Willy* must be one of those others. It had not been hard to discover her arrival date and time. It has been easy enough to find out where Port Vulcan was situated. It was on Vulcan Island, the location for New Venusberg's industries—apart from the tourist industry, of course. There was a regular air service to and from the industrial complex but it was rarely, if ever, used by tourists. Holiday makers had better (or worse) things to do with their time than the inspection of automated factories.

Fenella Pruin said that it might excite suspicion if she and Grimes proceeded to Port Vulcan by a scheduled flight to watch *Willy Willy*'s arrival. It would be quite in character, however, if she, playing the role of a bored rich bitch, hired a camperfly for a few days for a leisurely drift around the scenic beauties of the pleasure planet. The camperflies were smallish aircraft with sleeping accommodation and cooking and toilet facilities. They were hybrid machines with helium gas cells incorporated in their thick wings and above their fuselages, slow but airworthy, suitable for handling by amateur pilots. They were so buoyant that it was quite impossible for them to come down hard. The girl in the Uflyit office was only mildly interested when Grimes produced his Master Astronaut's Certificate of Competency as proof that he was a capable pilot. She was much more interested in seeing that Fenella Pruin paid the quite enormous but returnable deposit.

It was a fine morning when Grimes and his passenger lifted off from Port Aphrodite. He had spent most of the previous day accustoming himself to the controls of the rented aircraft and then had retired early. Fenella Pruin had spent the day and most of the night with Captain McKillick. McKillick, looking very much the worse for wear, came to the Uflyit landing field, on the outskirts of the spaceport apron, to see them off.

He glared at Grimes from bloodshot eyes.

He said, "You know that I could have taken a few days leave, Prue, to pilot you around . . ."

She said, "And leave Grimes, here, to carry on boozing and wenching at my expense? Not bloody likely. I'm making him earn his keep."

"But he doesn't have the local knowledge that I have."

"He can read a chart. And it isn't as though we're going anywhere in particular. We shall just be bumbling around."

The Port Captain turned on Grimes.

"Look after her," he threatened with a touching show of devotion, "or I'll have your guts for a necktie when you get back!"

"Mphm," Grimes grunted.

He stood to one side and watched McKillick try to enfold the girl in a loving embrace. She did not cooperate; the wet kiss that should have plastered itself over her mouth landed on her ear.

She broke away, saying, "I'll be seeing you, Jock. If you can't be good, be careful."

She clambered into the cabin of the tubby aircraft.

"Be seeing you, Captain," said Grimes.

"Be seeing you, Captain," replied McKillick with a distinct lack of enthusiasm.

The two men did not shake hands.

Grimes boarded and went forward, sat down beside Fenella Pruin. The aircraft was designed for easy handling with minimal controls. Trying to make it look even easier than it actually was Grimes went through the take-off procedure. The electric motors whined and the camperfly rose at a steep angle, obedient to Grimes' touch. He did not set course at once for Vulcan Island but circled the spaceport as he ascended, looking down at the ships both great and small, at his own *Little Sister* goldenly agleam in her berth between the huge TG liner and the big Shaara vessel. There was some activity around the latter. He wondered briefly what the bee people were doing; they seemed to be hauling something bulky out of a cargo airlock.

After his second circuit Fenella Pruin demanded irritably, "What are you playing at, Grimes? Trying to disappear up your own fundamental orifice?"

He told her, "We don't want to be seen heading for Vulcan Island."

"At the moment we aren't heading *anywhere*."

Grimes sighed resignedly and then, ignoring the compass, steered for a tall conical peak to the westward. The Mons Veneris Park would be as good an apparent destination as any; once he was out of sight from Port Aphrodite he would bring the camperfly around to a north easterly course. There was ample time to waste; allowing for two nocturnal set-downs they should be at Port Vulcan a good three hours prior to Aloysius Dreeble's ETA.

She said (couldn't she ever stop talking?), "You aren't such a bright businessman, you know."

"I know," he said. He thought, *If I were I wouldn't be obliged to carry people like you around.*

"If you were," she went on, "you'd do the same as the Shaara. Carry a blimp on board for this sort of outing."

"Where would I stow the bloody thing?" he snarled.

"Even you," she sneered, "might have more sense than to carry it with the gas cells inflated. But I suppose it would be beneath your precious dignity to learn anything from the Shaara."

"Why the sudden interest in those bloody bumblebees?" he demanded.

"It's just that we're being followed," she told him.

The pilot's cab of the camperfly was a transparent bubble set above fuselage top level, affording all-round vision. Grimes looked aft. Yes, there was something astern, coming up on them slowly. He could not be sure but it did look like a Shaara blimp. It had to be a Shaara blimp. As far as he knew there were no aircraft of that type native to New Venusberg.

"Are you going to let them pass us?" she asked.

He said, "I've no option. This camperfly is designed for comfort, not for speed."

"But a bloody gasbag . . ."

"Gasbag it may be but it's not starved for horsepower. Or workerpower, or whatever term the Shaara use."

"Don't be so bloody pedantic."

The camperfly flew on, still heading for the Mons Veneris. The blimp gained steadily on its parallel course, a little to starboard, flying at the same altitude as the humans' aircraft. Grimes studied it through the binoculars that were included in the rented equipment. He could see the arthropod crew in the open car under the envelope—a mixed bunch of drones and princesses he decided. Was *his* princess, the one with whom he had exchanged words in Lady Luck's establishment, among them? he wondered. She might be. And so what? Presumably the ban on the carrying of weapons on this world applied to all visitors, not only to human beings. And what could unarmed Shaara do to him?

They could get in his hair, that was what.

The blimp was abeam of the camperfly now, matching speed, blocking Grimes' turn on to the north easterly course. Its crew were watching him through their big, faceted eyes. Sunlight was reflected dazzlingly from the jewels that adorned the dark brown, velvety fur of their bodies.

But ships of the air are not like surface vehicles; they have freedom to move in three dimensions. Grimes made a rude, two fingered gesture to the watching Shaara, put the camperfly into a shallow dive as he turned to starboard. It was the easiest maneuver to carry out in these circumstances; it also turned out to be a foolish one.

The camperfly was directly under the airship when Grimes realised this. For the secod time during his stay on New Venusberg he was bombed by the Shaara. A shower of missiles fell from the blimp's car, clattering on to the transparent canopy of the cab, thudding on to the tough plastic containing the wing and fuselage gas cells. The camperfly staggered, heeled over dangerously. The heavy object that had landed on the starboard wing tip and stayed there fell off but not before Grimes had seen what it was, one of those large earthenware containers referred to as honeypots, a jar in which the Shaara had carried semi-fluid refreshment to sustain them during their trip.

"What the bloody hell?" screamed Fenella Pruin.

"Somebody up there doesn't like us," muttered Grimes.

But there was no damage to the camperfly. Although some of the jetsam had been heavy none of it had been sharp. A container of some kind had shattered on top of the bubble canopy and overhead vision was obscured by a red, syrupy mess. Through it, dimly, Grimes could see the blimp. It was now little more than a dot in the sky. After that dumping of weight it had gone up fast.

"And just what was all that about?" demanded the girl.

"The Shaara—these particular Shaara—have it in for me."

"And so I'm liable to suffer for your misdeeds."

"I'm here too."

"More's the pity. Anyhow, what do you intend doing about it?"

"We just carry on," said Grimes, "until it's time to land for the night."

"And get bombed again."

"I don't think so," he said. "My guess—for what it's worth—is that the Shaara are keeping an eye on me. A surveillance mission only. But that princess, seizing a heaven sent opportunity to be nasty, just gathered up everything dumpable in the car and dropped it on us. Just petty spite."

"It could have been serious."

"It wasn't."

"The surveillance—if your theory is correct—is. I don't want to be snooped on."

"The biter bit," said Grimes.

"Oh, shut up!" Then, after a pause, "And what are you *doing* about it?"

"I'll think of something," said Grimes with a confidence that he did not feel.

The Shaara blimp kept them company throughout the day. Grimes could not outrun it. The arthropods, however, took no further hostile action; presumably they had nothing else that they could afford to jettison. But it was not a happy flight for Grimes and his companion; they were continually and uncomfortably aware of hostile eyes looking down on them.

As already planned they came in to Camp Diana in the afternoon. Before they landed the Shaara airship sheered off, vanishing beyond a range of low, wooded hills to the northward. Perhaps it was returning to the spaceport, as Fenella Pruin suggested. Grimes did not think so. He feared that they would be seeing more of the arthropods before arrival at Vulcan Island.

Camp Diana was situated on the south bank of the narrow river. There was a little hill overlooking the broad meadow upon which camperflies and pneumatic tents were arranged in orderly lines and upon this eminence was a silver statue of the divine huntress, bow in hand. The artist had depicted a lady who, despite her archaic armament, looked to be more versed in bedroom venery than the outdoor sport for which the same word is used. She did not have at all the appearance of a virgin goddess. By the water's edge was the hunting lodge, so called. It was a large, white building of vaguely classical architecture. On its roof was a mast with a windsock that was hanging limply in the calm, warm air. There was, too, a squat control tower and from this Grimes received his landing instructions.

He set down in a vacant space in one of the lines of camperflies, making an almost vertical descent. He watched from the cab a young woman walking out to the aircraft, looked at her appreciatively. She was dressed in filmy *chiton* that left one breast bare and that revealed most of her long, slender legs. The effect of her pseudo-Grecian attire, however, was slighly marred by a very modern looking shoulder bag. (She had to have something, thought Grimes cynically, in which she stowed the money, camping fees and the like, that she collected from the customers.)

She waited at the door of the camperfly for Grimes and Fenella Pruin to emerge. She said, her voice high and silvery, "Welcome to Camp Diana." Then, "For how long do you intend to stay, sir and miss?"

"Only for the night," Grimes told her.

"Only for the night, sir? But you will miss tomorrow's hunt. Perhaps you will reconsider. This evening you will have ample time for arbalest instruction at the range in the lodge basement . . ."

"What the hell's an arbalest?" demanded Fenella Pruin.

"A crossbow," said Grimes. "Its great advantage over the longbow is that little training is required before a bowman is reasonably competent."

"But *weapons*," persisted Fenella. "After all the fuss you had with the Customs at Port Aphrodite I got the impression that weapons were banned on this world."

"They are, miss," the girl told her. "But for a deer hunt bows must be used—longbows for the few capable of employing them, arbalests for those who must learn archery in a hurry. They are hired from the lodge and during the hunt strict supervision is exercised." She smiled. "In the extremely unlikely event of any of our guests not returning his bow before leaving the camp he will find it of little use save as a souvenir. After all, it is not a concealed weapon. It is not the sort of thing that one can carry into a cathouse or gambling den unnoticed. In fact if a bow is carried anywhere save in the precincts of a hunting camp such as this it will at once excite the interest of the authorities." She took time off to recover her breath then continued, "Have I persuaded you to stay for the hunt, sir?"

"I'm afraid not," said Grimes. "But I should like to get in some arbalest practice this evening."

"What the hell for?" demanded Fenella Pruin.

"We might enjoy a longer stay here next time we drop in."

"Oh, well, if that's your idea of a pleasant evening, go ahead. I'm not stopping you. But you pay for your own tuition; I'm not subsidizing your fun. It's bad enough having to shell out for camping fees. How much do I owe for one night?" she asked the girl. "*What?* Oh, well, this *is* a hunting camp. You're the predator and we're the prey . . ."

She went back into the camperfly for money. Grimes looked at the girl. She looked at him. Two pairs of eyebrows were raised simultaneously.

Grimes asked, "What time are these arbalest lessons?"

"Any time you like," she said. "Do you plan on shooting her—accidentally, of course?"

"Mphm," grunted Grimes noncommitally.

Grimes demanded money.

Fenella Pruin asked, "What for? For an arbalest lesson? Your Survey Service gunnery courses can't have cost all that much!"

"I may want to grease a palm or two," he said.

She looked at him. She said slowly, "I think I can guess why. But I'm not asking. I don't want to know anything about it. I refuse to accept responsibility for any illegality of which you may be guilty."

"Unfortunately," said Grimes, "as master I cannot do likewise as far as you are concerned."

"Here's your money," she said, concluding the conversation. She peeled notes of large denominations off the large roll that she produced from her bag.

Grimes counted what she gave him. It should be enough, more than enough. He left the camperfly, walked in the late-afternoon sunlight to the lodge.

He found his way to the practice range with no trouble. Apart from the attendant on duty, a young lady got up to conform to somebody's idea of what a well dressed Amazon should wear—leather straps, brass buckles, an extremely short kilt of some transparent material—the practice range was deserted. She looked at Grimes and smiled invitingly.

"Archery instruction, sir? Or . . ."

"Archery instruction, please."

The smile faded slightly.

"Longbow or arbalest, sir?"

"Arbalest, please."

"Have you used such a weapon before?"

"No."

"In that case, sir, you will require the stimulator if you are to acquire a modicum of skill in the minimum time. It was programmed by Hiroshi Hayashi, for many years the undisputed crossbow champion of all Venusberg." She added, after a slight pause, "There will be an extra charge, of course."

"Of course," agreed Grimes.

He was led to a long counter of polished wood. Beyond this, at a distance of about forty metres, was a large target with a bullseye and concentric rings. From under the bar the girl produced a crossbow, put the end of it on the floor and one slim foot into the stirrup, grasped the wire bowstring with both hands—it was suitably padded in the two places necessary—and pulled. There was a click as the sear engaged. She lifted the weapon, put it back on the counter and then inserted a steel quarrel into the slot. Then, with the butt of the arbalest set firmly on her right shoulder, she took casual aim and pulled the trigger. The bowstring twanged musically and the target thudded as the metal bolt sank deep into the bullseye.

It all looked very easy.

"And now you, sir. Cock, load and fire."

It had all looked very easy when she did it but Grimes was amazed at the effort required to bend those steel arms. He was red in the face and perspiring when finally the thing was cocked. He loaded. He brought the butt to his shoulder. The weapon was too heavy and the balance was all wrong. He tried to steady the primitive sights on to the target but could not hold the crossbow steady. He pulled the trigger at last when his foresight flickered across the bullseye. He missed, of course, not even putting the quarrel on to the quite large target.

The girl *tsked* sympathetically. She brought from its under the counter stowage a featureless helmet of some light metal. She set it firmly on Grimes' head.

"Now, sir, cock, load and fire."

It had all looked very easy when she did it. It was surprisingly easy when he did it—this time. It was as though something— somebody—had control of his brain, was telling his muscles exactly what they should do. (This stimulator, he thought, must use a very similar technique to that employed by that obscene game machine in Lady Luck's games machines room.) He pulled up the bowspring until it engaged with an amazing lack of effort. He raised the arbalest to his shoulder, sighted carelessly, fired. He was well on the target this time although missing the bullseye by a few millimetres. He cocked, reloaded, fired again. A bull. Cock, reload, fire . . . Another bull. And another. Dislodged quarrels fell to the stone floor with a clatter.

This was not, thought Grimes, the quickfiring weapon that a longbow was. Even with his induced skills reloading took too much time.

He asked, "Could I learn to use a longbow the same way?"

"Yes, sir. But it takes much longer. You, obviously, are accustomed to handling projectile firearms employing a chemical propellant. This technique is merely enhancing the skills that you already possess . . ."

And a crossbow, thought Grimes, would be easier to fire from the open door of an aircraft. He would stay with it.

At the girl's suggestion he switched to moving targets, two dimensional representations of animals that had to be Terran deer, their ancestral stock no doubt imported from Earth. These ran rapidly from left to right, from right to left, bobbed up suddenly.

He scored well after a shaky start.

She said, "You will bring back game from tomorrow's hunt, sir."

"I shan't be at tomorrow's hunt."

"The day after, perhaps . . . I must warn you that unless you practice continuously the induced skills fade."

"Could I take two of these arbalests back to my camperfly so that I and my companion can get in some practice?"

"It is not allowed, sir. Our weapons may be used only under strict supervision."

"You must have occasional outworld tourists," suggested Grimes, "who want to keep these beautiful crossbows as souvenirs . . ."

"They are expensive," said the girl bluntly. At least she wasn't wasting time by being coy.

"How much?" asked Grimes, equally bluntly.

"Five hundred credits each. And I must warn you that if you are seen carrying one anywhere but within the bounds of a camp such as this you will be liable to arrest and prosecution. And if you say that you bought it you will not be believed. We have an understanding with the police forces. You will be charged with theft as well as carrying an unauthorised weapon."

"You're certainly frank," said Grimes, looking at the girl not without approval. He had his notecase out, was checking its contents. "Now I'm going to be frank. I haven't enough on me to pay for the arbalests *and* the tuition. And my . . . er . . . friend keeps very tight pursestrings . . ." He tried to look like a gigolo. "Perhaps . . ."

"How much have you got?"

"One thousand, five hundred and seventy five . . ."

She grinned. "Near enough."

He should have tried to beat her down, thought Grimes. But it wasn't his money. It wasn't even Fenella Pruin's money. *The Bronson Star* could well afford it.

Shortly thereafter, with the dissembled arbalests and a supply of quarrels in a carrying case that the girl had thrown in with the purchase, he made his way through the warm dusk to the camperfly.

Fenella Pruin, although reluctantly approving this acquisition of weaponry, was not at all pleased when he insisted that she learn how to cock and load a crossbow.

These were not quick-firing weapons—but if things came to a crunch they would have to do.

Eleven

The next morning, after a light breakfast that Grimes prepared from the camperfly's consumable stores, they lifted from Camp Diana. A bored duty officer in the control tower asked them where they were bound and was told that they were just cruising. (On most worlds they would have been obliged to submit a flight plan before departure but New Venusberg concerned itself only about the ability of tourists to pay for their pleasure.) The flight controller told them to have a happy day. Grimes thanked him—and wondered if the day would be a happy one. He hoped that it would be.

He flew with the rising sun broad on the starboard bow, its brilliance reduced to a tolerable level by the self-polarising glass of the cockpit canopy. Dazzle was cut down but so, inevitably, was visibility. But he was sure that attack, if there were to be an attack, would come from out of the sun.

It did.

At first the Shaara blimp was no more than a sunspot, but a rapidly expanding one. Grimes put the controls on automatic, said to Fenella Pruin, "This is it. Are you ready?"

"Yes," she said. "But I forbid you to open fire unless they start dropping things again . . ."

"They'll have spent the night," Grimes told her, "gathering big stones with sharp edges."

"You don't *know* . . ."

"I don't *know*—but would you like to bet that they haven't?"

She made no reply and he began to remove the nuts—which he had already loosened to hand tightness only—holding the rear panel of the canopy in place. Unfortunately there was no room for the segment of curved glass inside the cockpit but Grimes had foreseen this, had ready some light but very strong line that, passed through the bolt holes of the removed panel and those in an adjacent one, held it more or less securely. The thing tended to flap in the wind of the camperfly's passage; if the cord frayed through it would be just too bad.

Meanwhile the blimp was no longer a sunspot; it was

eclipsing the sun. The Shaara were on a collision course but Grimes was sure that they would lift before there was actual contact. They did so, and by this time Grimes was half way out of the bubble canopy and on to the smooth, resilient top of the gas cell that covered the fuselage. He held one of the arbalests, already cocked and loaded, ready for action. The other one Fenella Pruin would pass to him as soon as he needed it.

He edged out to starboard, putting a cautious foot on to the root of the stubby wing on that side. He withdrew hastily, back to the protection of the canopy. Even at the camperfly's low air speed there was too much wind; he would never be able to take steady aim and, furthermore, would run the serious risk of losing his balance and falling. It was a long way down and the terrain over which they were now flying was rocky. (Even had it been soft sand he would never have survived such a plunge.)

So he would have to follow the Pruin's orders (but what right had *she* to order *him*?) after all. He would not be able to open fire until fired upon. His missiles going up would pass the Shaara missiles coming down.

The blimp had reduced speed as it gained altitude and then, to Grimes' surprise, sheered off to port.

"You've gone to all this trouble for nothing," sneered Fenella Pruin. "They aren't going to attack us. Why should they? And how am I going to justify the purchase of these two bloody crossbows to my paper?"

"Wait!" snapped Grimes.

The blimp was astern of them now, but it was turning. It was coming up on them slowly, on the same course as themselves but higher. When the Shaara started dropping things they would have to make very little allowance for deflection. Their tactics were ideal assuming that the bombing target was unarmed. Grimes hastily put the arbalest behind his back. If they saw the glint of metal they would suspect that he had a weapon of some kind.

The camperfly flew on steadily.

The blimp crept up on it.

It would be, thought Grimes, just within the extreme range of his arbalest. But was that bloody Fenella Pruin telepathic?

"Wait!" she ordered sharply. "Let them make the first move!"

"It may be the last as far as we're concerned," he replied but kept the crossbow concealed.

The fat nose of the blimp was directly above the camperfly's stubby tail. Sunlight was reflected dazzlingly from the jewels worn by the princesses and drones in the car, from their faceted eyes. They must be wondering what Grimes was doing standing out on the fuselage. They would soon find out.

The obese airship slowly overflew the chubby hybrid aircraft. The car was coming directly overhead. Grimes saw spindly, arthropoidal limbs, holding things, extending outward from the gondola. The first missiles were released. He did not watch their descent but whipped the arbalest up from behind his back and fired, aiming for the rear of the car where the engine driving the pusher airscrew was situated. He missed, but the quarrel drove into and through the envelope. He heard, behind him, at least one rock crashing on to the cockpit canopy, felt the camperfly lurch dangerously as others hit the wings. But there was no time to assess damage. He passed the discharged arbalest back to Fenella Pruin, grabbed the loaded one that she put into his hand. He brought the butt to his shoulder and fired just as another shower of big stones came down. The blimp was still within range; it should not have been, that first act of jettison should have sent it climbing almost like a rocket.

Grimes realised why as his second bolt sped towards its intended target. The first one must have hit some weak spot, a juncture of gas cells. Tattered fabric flapped about a widening rent in the envelope. The airship was dropping by the stern. Unless Grimes took avoiding action, and fast, it would fall on to the camperfly.

Fantastically the hybrid aircraft was looking after itself. It swung around to starboard at the same time as it heeled over in that direction and the sinking blimp dropped slowly astern of it, just missing its tail. Grimes realised almost at once the reason for the alteration of course; the gas cell in the starboard wing had been holed and the automatic pilot had been unable to cope with the change in trim. And Grimes himself would be unable to cope until matters of far greater urgency had been resolved.

Two of the Shaara, a princess and a drone, had bailed out from their crippled vehicle. They were making for the almost as crippled camperfly. Grimes did not have to be psychic to know that they were in a bad temper. Probably they were unarmed but they would be able to inflict considerable damage with their sharp talons.

He retreated inside the canopy.

Fenella Pruin was still struggling to reload the first arbalest. He snatched it from her and, the training session not yet faded from his mind, cocked the thing without difficulty. He watched the two Shaara, their wings an iridescent blue, flying in. There was not sufficient slipstream from the slow camperfly seriously to interfere with their landing. Using all their limbs they scuttled forward to where Grimes, crossbow in hand, awaited them. They came erect on their rear legs before they reach him.

The princess said, her voice from the artificial speech box strapped to her thorax viciously strident, "You have a weapon. On this world it is not legal."

"Neither is dropping rocks on people," Grimes told her.

"You broke the law. We are entitled to protect ourselves against lawbreakers."

"Try it!" he said, levelling the arbalest.

But would he dare to use it? So far action had been taken, by both sides, against ships only. Intentions and results had been damage to property, not to life and limb. If he killed the princess or the drone, or both of them, the other Shaara would lay formal complaint to the Venusberg authorities and then Grimes would be in the cactus. The Shaara pulled more Gs on this world than he did. He did not know what the penalty was for the crime of murder but he did not doubt that it would be extremely unpleasant.

Yet without the weapon he would be no match for the multi-limbed, sharp clawed arthropod. Perhaps (he hoped) the threat of its use would be sufficient to deter the Shaara from unarmed attack.

They approached him slowly, meanacingly, their clawed feet clinging to the taut fabric of the upper fuselage gas cell. Grimes' finger tightened on the trigger of the arbalest.

Behind him something hissed loudly.

A stream of white foam shot over his shoulder, played over the head of the princess and then over that of her companion, blinding them. Fortuitously the camperfly lurched heavily at this moment. The princess screeched wordlessly, lost her balance and fell overside. She was in no danger; her wings opened at once and she was airborne but flying aimlessly, all sense of direction lost. The drone still stood there, trying to clear the viscous foam from his eyes. Grimes took a cautious step aft towards him, pushed hard with the crossbow held in his right hand. The drone staggered but the claws of his feet

retained their grip. Grimes jabbed again, and again. He was
afraid of injuring the male Shaara but was anxious to be rid of
him.

Then a metal cylinder, thrown with force and accuracy
from somewhere behind him, struck the drone on the thorax.
He staggered, lost his footing, fell to join his aimlessly flying
mistress.

Grimes turned cautiously to make his way back to the
control cab. Fenella Pruin was standing in the opening made
by the removed panel, grinning happily.

"If *they* can dump used food containers and the like," she
said, "*I* can dump used fire extinguishers."

"If they complain," he said, "we're still in trouble."

"Nobody was killed," she told him. "That wouldn't have
been so if you'd used the crossbow."

Grimes reluctantly agreed with her and then went to the
pilot's seat to try to bring the camperfly back under control.

He was obliged to valve gas from the port wing to compensate for the loss of lift from the starboard one. The camperfly
was still airworthy but with the reduction of buoyancy there
was a corresponding reduction of speed. The necessary calcu-
lations would have to wait, however, until the canopy panel
was replaced. Grimes felt much happier when the control cab
was once again completely enclosed, affording protection
against an incursion of vengeful Shaara.

The cockpit resealed, he took his place at the controls,
studied the chart on the desk before him.

He said, "We'll make Camp Persephone all right, although
a bit later than intended. There are sure to be repair facilities
there and a supply of helium. We'll get the starboard wing
patched up and both wing gas cells refilled."

"How will you account for the hole in the starboard wing?"

He grinned at her. "I'm just a spaceman. You're the
writer. Use your imagination."

She grinned back. "I'll just soft pedal the truth a little. We
happened to be flying directly under a Shaara blimp when,
quite by chance, the thing dumped ballast. We don't want to
have to lay any charges. The less the law knows about our
activities here, the better."

To tell the truth, although not necessarily the whole truth,
is usually safer than to tell a lie.

Twelve

———◆———

Camp Persephone was hot springs and fumaroles, dominated by a spectacular geyser, spouting with clockwork regularity every thirteen and a half minutes. There was a huge hotel complex for those wishing to make an extended stay and a big camperfly park with the usual facilities, including a repair shop. To this Grimes went almost immediately after landing, taking with him what he hoped would be an adequate supply of *The Bronson Star*'s money.

The manager was just shutting up shop.

He was oilily courteous, however.

"Repairs to your camperfly, sir, at this time of the evening? My staff have all left for the night and I was on the point of leaving . . . But I have no doubt, sir, that we shall be able to make an arrangement, a mutually satisfactory arrangement . . ."

"It is a matter of some urgency," said Grimes.

"Of course, sir." He coughed delicately. "Forgive me for my impertinence but now and again—very rarely, but now and again—we have tourists who are not your sort of people, who demand services and then who are unable or unwilling to give recompense in return . . ."

"So you want to see the colour of my money," said Grimes crudely.

"Ha, ha. You have a ready wit, sir . . ."

"And ready cash." Grimes brought out and opened his notecase.

"What is the trouble with your camperfly, sir?"

"The starboard wing gas cell was holed. I was obliged to valve gas from the port wing to compensate."

"An unusual accident, sir, perhaps you were flying too low and fouled a tree top or some other obstacle . . ."

"Perhaps," said Grimes.

He walked with the manager through the sulphur-tainted evening air along the lines of parked camperflies. He took the man into the aircraft, up to the canopied cockpit, shone a

torch on to the jagged rent in the wing fabric. He said, "The
. . . er . . . obstacle is still inside the wing."

"But were you flying *upside down*, sir?"

"I was trying to loop the loop," said Grimes.

The manager stared at him, then said, "The most peculiar
accidents do happen, I know. If you will wait here, sir, until I
recall my staff . . . But, if you will forgive my impertinence,
first a small deposit before I do so . . ."

Grimes paid up. After all, it wasn't his money.

The repair job did not take long. The piece of jagged rock
was removed from the punctured gas cell. The repair shop
manager was sorely puzzled but Grimes stuck to his looping
the loop story. Improbable as it was it was better than the one
suggested by Fenella Pruin. Disposable ballast carried by
airships is never of a character likely to damage anything or
anybody underneath . . .

The repairmen worked well and efficiently. The damaged
cell was removed and replaced, and inflated before the re-
newal of wing fabric. The gas cell in the port wing was
reinflated and tested. When everything was done Grimes paid
the balance of the charges and was relieved to find that when
he had asked Fenella Pruin for the money he had slightly
overestimated. He made a light meal of cheese and biscuits,
then went in search of his passenger so that he could report
that the next day's journey would be as planned. She would
be in the hotel, he thought, probably eating far better than he
had done. But she must have fed by now. Hadn't she said
something about paying a visit to The Inferno later in the
evening?

So, with wallet much lighter but not empty, he left the
camperfly and walked towards the Hotel Pluto, a fantastic
appearing building whose architect had taken stalagmites as
his inspiration, whose irregular spires, floodlit, were whitely
luminous against the night sky. Off to the right the geyser—
also floodlit but in rainbow colours—momentarily distracted
his attention from the man-made extravagance.

He reached the grotto-like entrance to the hotel, passed into
a cavernous foyer where artificial stalactites and stalagmites
dominated the decor. There were luminous signs—one of
which, by an ascending spiral escalator, read Elysian Fields
Restaurant and another, over what looked like a mere hole in
the floor, The Inferno.

By the hole was the inevitable pay booth, a construction looking like a huge dog kennel made from rough, rock slabs. The attendant wore a ferocious dog mask and nothing else. But, so far as Grimes could remember, Cerberus had been a male dog and not a bitch. (And, in any case, the idea of Hell as an inferno was a Christian invention and bore little resemblance to the Greek Hades.)

He paid his not inconsiderable sop to Cerberus. He asked if there would be any ferry fees as an additional charge and was told that there would not be, although as soon as the proposed artificial Styx was flowing there would be fares collected by Charon.

Grimes thanked the girl. He wondered if her face were as attractive as her voice and body. He went to look dubiously into the hole. There was no staircase, either static or mobile. It was just a chute of black, polished stone, plunging downwards at a steep angle.

Rather dubiously Grimes sat down on the rim with his legs in the hole, then pushed off. At first his descent was almost free fall, through utter darkness. The acridity of sulphurous gases stung his nostrils. Then he felt that the angle of the chute was less steep, was tending to the horizontal. His speed was checked by a screen of curtains that clung like cobwebs. Beyond them there was light again—ruddy, flickering, but to eyes that had become accustomed to the darkness bright enough.

He had come to a halt on a smooth floor of rock, or artificial rock. He got to his feet, looked around. Slowly swirling luminously crimson mist restricted visiblity but he could dimly see stalactites and stalagmites—or, more probably, plastic representations of dribbles of molten lava that had solidified on reaching the ground, like candle drippings on a giant scale. The air was hot and steamy. There was music. It was vaguely familiar in spite of the distortions. *Night On Bald Mountain?* Grimes couldn't be sure but he thought that it was that.

A demon materialised beside him. Gleaming white horns—probably artificial but not necessarily so; unscrupulous genetic engineers are capable of many amusing perversions—protruded jauntily from her cap of tightly curled black hair. Grimes allowed his regard to shift downward. Her body was human enough except for the feet, which were cloven hooves. Shoes? Perhaps. But if they were her pedal extremities must have been exceedingly small to get into them.

"May I serve you, sir?" Her voice was a pleasant contralto. He could not place the accent.

"I'm looking for a lady . . ."

"There are many unattached ladies here, sir."

"A tourist. A Miss Fenn. Prunella Fenn."

"She is not known to me, sir. But probably she will be in the Lake of Fire. If you will follow me . . ."

She turned away from him. He saw that a scaly tail, terminating in a conventional arrowhead, sprouted jauntily from the cleft of her naked buttocks. He could not resist the temptation of catching hold of it, giving it a playful tug. The root of it came away from her body, snapped back when he released his hold. She looked back with a smile that was wearily tolerant rather than pleasant; having her tail pulled must have been an occupational hazard of her employment.

"Artificial caudal appendages may be purchased here. They are ideal for fancy dress parties and the like. But come with me, please."

He followed her through the acrid yet sweet mists to a small, pallidly glimmering pavilion where she handed him over to another woman attired—horns, hooves and tail—as she was. This lady told him to remove his clothing, then asked for a fee, not a small one, in return for a locker key which was on a chain so that it could be hung about the neck. She asked Grimes if he wished to buy or hire horns and a tail. He did not so wish even though he was assured that these embellishments would enhance his manly beauty. Before he stowed and locked his possessions away the first girl intimated that she was expecting a tip. Grimes gave her a ten credit bill; there was nothing of smaller denomination in his notecase. He thought that it was too much. She, obviously, did not.

Nonetheless she condescended to lead him from the pavilion to the edge of the Lake of Fire. Streamers of mist wavering above the surface of the sullenly glowing water had the semblance of tongues of flame. And there were real flames, yellow and not red, out there in the distance, seemingly floating on the surface, like a star cluster dimly glimpsed through the fire mist of some inchoate nebula.

"Your lady is out there," said the guide, pointing. "If she's here, that is."

"Do I have to swim?" asked Grimes.

"Only if you wish to."

Grimes tested the temperature of the water at the lake verge with a cautious toe. It was little more than comfortably warm. He waded out towards the glimmering lights. As he disturbed the surface it flashed brightly scarlet, illuminating the mist that swirled about him. It was like walking through fire—but a fire that had no power to burn.

He waded on. The bottom shelved gently; still the water was only half way up to his knees. He thought at first that the lambent flames were receding from him as he headed towards them but this was only some trick of refraction. Quite suddenly—by which time the water was up to his knees—he was among them. He looked down with some bewilderment at the naked men and women obviously sitting on the lake bottom each with a tray, on which was a burning candle, floating before him or her. The trays bore more than candles. There were bottles, glasses, dishes of solid refreshments.

And where was Fenella Pruin?

He looked to right and left but could not see her. But he heard her unmistakable voice, off somewhere to the right. She was complaining loudly to somebody, "Isn't it time that they put on the next show? I can't stay here much longer. I want to get some sleep tonight as I shall be leaving early in the morning—if my fool of a pilot has had my camperfly repaired, that is . . ."

He waded slowly towards her, rippling the water. Somebody called to him irritably, "Hey, you! Don't rock the boat!"

He reduced his speed. He had no wish to spill people's drinks. He apologised when he trod on a bare leg under the water, smilingly refused the invitation to sit down and keep its owner, a plump tourist lady, company.

He found Fenella Pruin. She was with a grossly fat man who could almost have been twin brother to Captain McKillick, who had stuck on to his bald head a pair of patently artificial horns. Before them was a large, floating tray laden with good things.

The big toe of Grimes' right foot made contact with Miss Pruin's naked hip.

"Who the hell . . .?" she began.

"It's your fool of a pilot," said Grimes.

"Oh. You." She looked up at him. "What do you want?"

"The camperfly's airworthy again. We shall be able to lift off tomorrow morning as planned."

"It's a pity that you have to leave, Prue," sighed the fat man. "Just when . . ."

Grimes looked down at his obese, pallid nudity. First McKillick, he thought, and now this overweight slob. And he must have some skin disease; if a cross between a Terran leopard and a hippopotamus were possible he could have been it.

"Sit down, Grimes," snarled the Pruin. "Since you're here you can watch the second show and then see me back to the camperfly."

"But, Prue . . ." The fat man's voice was childishly plaintive.

"Sorry, Clarrie. But I'm paying Grimes, here, good money to look after me—and I like getting my money's worth."

"So do I," muttered her companion.

Grimes lowered his body into the warm water on the other side of Fenella Pruin from Clarrie. If whatever caused that ugly, mottled skin was catching he didn't want to catch it. Almost immediately one of the attendant demons appeared; this one was towing, by her tail, a little, flatbottomed barge. From it she took a tray, with a candle, set it before Grimes, ignited the wick with a flick of her long finger nails. By its light Grimes read the menu and the wine list printed on the surface of the tray. Unless the Pruin came to his rescue he would not be able to afford much. Beer would be the cheapest drink. (Here it was called Teufelwasser.) But how, naked as he was, could he pay for it?

He found out. Having set the bottle and glass on his tray the girl took a stamp and pressed it on his right upper arm. It left, in indelible ink, a record of what he had ordered and received. Presumably there would be a reckoning in the pavilion when he retrieved his effects. He looked at the sulking, mottled Clarrie. He felt almost sorry for the man; his skin bore the record of his evening's outlay on the ungrateful Pruin.

Grimes sipped his beer—it wasn't bad—and looked around. The mists were clearing and he could see that the audience was seated in a great circle with a low island in its centre. This was flat, bare of vegetation. Suddenly, appearing from the mouth of a concealed tunnel, a horde of fearsome looking demons appeared, Neanderthalers with cloven hooves, horns and tails, with leathery wings. Moving in time to the music they set up their horrifying apparatus—a rack, a brazier from which protruded the handles of branding irons, a wheel from the rim of which protruded vicious, dull-gleaming spikes. At a wave from a taloned hand the brazier came to glowing life.

From overhead came a rumble of thunder, culminating in a supernal *crack* while artificial lightning flared dazzlingly. Spiralling down from the high roof of the cavern, wings outspread, came more demons. (Those wings, thought Grimes, were all wrong aerodynamically; they were not moving and, in any case, did not have the area to support anything as large as a man, let alone a man burdened with a struggling woman. Miniaturised, personal inertial drive units? Probably. The continuous grumble of thunder, combined with the strident music, was loud enough to drown the arhythmic beat of such machinery.)

Dark-furred demons with pallidly gleaming eyes and tusks and horns . . . Shrieking, damned women, their opulent flesh whitely naked, fighting but with utter hopelessness. One of them was flung roughly on to the rack, her wrists and ankles strapped. Another was made fast to the wheel. ("Watch those spikes," whispered Fenella Pruin. "They aren't sharp and they withdraw into the rim.") Two more were chained to St Andrew's crosses.

"You must let me take you to the real thing, Prue," muttered the fat man. "This is *tame* . . ."

"Shut up!" she snapped.

And this, thought Grimes, looked real enough. With two husky demons manning the capstan the screaming girl on the rack was being elongated so that she looked more like a writhing, white snake than a human being, as was her sister on the wheel. Irons, whitely incandescent at first, slowly dulling to red, were being applied to the bodies of the crucified victims. There was an audible sizzling and the sweet/acrid stench of burning meat.

Grimes watched in horrified fascination. Towards the end he found it hard to fight down his rising nausea—and hated himself when he became aware that something else was rising too.

At last the show was almost over.

The girls were released from the rack, wheel and crosses, flung on to the ground where the demons, each of whom was more than adequately endowed, fell upon them. These withdrew at last, leaving the victims of the pack rape sprawled on the smooth rock.

The woman who had been on the rack was the first to recover. She sat up, stripped from her arms the stretched simulacra of her natural limbs and then, from her legs, what looked now only like ludicrously long hip-length stockings.

The victim of the wheel followed suit. Meanwhile, solicitously, two demons with damp white towels were cleaning the simulated burn-marks from the bodies of the other two girls.

The demons and the damned bowed to the audience, acknowledged the applause.

"Phoney," muttered the fat man. "Phoney as all hell. I know a place . . ."

"I'm sure you do, Clarrie." Fenella Pruin got to her feet, looked down at Grimes. "If you've quite finished your beer we'll get back to the camperfly."

They waded ashore, retrieved their clothing from the pavilion. The woman in charge raised her eyebrows at the solitary price stamp on Grimes' skin, accepted his money and handed him a wad of cloth impregnated with some fluid with which to remove the mark. Grimes dressed. Prunella Fenn dressed. They walked to the golden, spiral escalator that carried them back to ground level.

She said, "A pity we have to be at Port Vulcan. Otherwise I'd have taken Clarrie up on his offer. He's stinking rich— *really* stinking rich—you know and has the entré to all sorts of places that the ordinary rich, like I'm supposed to be, can't afford . . ."

"You wouldn't," said Grimes.

"I would. Too right I would. But I'll find a way yet . . ."

They left the hotel, made their way to the camperfly park.

Back in the aircraft they retired for what was left of the night.

Grimes was acutely aware that she was sleeping, probably naked, on the other side of the curtain dividing the cabin. Almost he got off his bunk to go to join her; that crudely sadistic and pornographic entertainment had stimulated him. Then he remembered what had happened (what had not happened) with her before and desire ebbed.

He tried to sleep and at last succeeded.

Thirteen

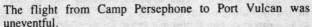

The flight from Camp Persephone to Port Vulcan was uneventful.

An early start was made, with Grimes, after a mug of strong coffee, feeling reasonably competent and his passenger still snoring not unmusically in her bunk. Grimes set course at once for Vulcan Island. Soon he was flying over the sea, looking down with interest at the waterborne traffic—a huge tanker (and what was she carrying? he wondered), a large, white-painted cruiser liner, a fleet of big trawlers.

Vulcan Island showed up on schedule, a dark smudge of smoke on the far horizon under which there was the glint of metal, the reflection of the morning sunlight from storage tanks, separator towers and the like. By this time Fenella Pruin was up and dressed, sitting beside Grimes as he maintained his course.

Grimes called Aerospace Control.

"Camperfly Able Zulu Steven Four Eight, pilot John Grimes, passenger Prunella Fenn, requesting permission to land."

"Vulcan Control to Able Zulu Seven Four Eight. I have you in my screen. You'll not be in time for today's tour of the dolly factory. You should have come in last night."

"Are there any entertainments that we can take in?" asked Grimes.

"Not until tomorrow. But come in if you want to. There'll be a berth for you at the airport."

Grimes looked at the Vulcan Island chart. Airport and spaceport were well away from each other. He measured off the distance—four kilometres. If there were no transport available the distance would not be too far to walk. But there might be, he thought, another problem. Very often ports frequented only by non-passenger-carrying vessels were sealed areas, with gates and guards and all the rest of it. But he had made plans for such a contingency. Aboard the camperfly were two suits of uniform-like coveralls, two hard hats (the design of this plastic safety headwear seemed to be standardised

75

throughout the Galaxy) and, most important of all, two clipboards. Also there was a pair of wirecutters.

He homed on the airport radio beacon.

He came in low, flying over the low, sprawling factory buildings, only one of which exhibited a splash of incongruous colour, a huge, pinkly naked, yellow-haired woman-shaped balloon floating above it. Perhaps it was not so incongruous after all. This must be the dolly factory mentioned by Vulcan Control.

The airport was an almost featureless square of grey concrete. There were three big passenger carriers in, inertial drive jobs. Tucked away in a corner were the camperflies, a half dozen of them. As instructed Grimes made his landing close by these hybrid aircraft.

A bored official sauntered out from the administration tower, waited for Grimes and Fenella Pruin to step down from the camperfly to the apron. He was mainly interested in collecting dues and charges.

Fenella Pruin asked, "What can we *do* here?"

"There's the conducted tour of the dolly factory, of course." The man leered. "Most of the fun is testing the dollies; they come in two sexes, you know. Apart from that there's Vulcan City. The shopping's not bad, they tell me. You save a few cents by buying your souvenirs here instead of at the mainland clipjoint shops."

"Could we just sort of wander around?" asked the girl.

"Sure. But outside Vulcan City there's little to see. The spaceport and the factories are out of bounds unless you have a pass."

"Shopping, darling?" suggested Miss Pruin, aiming a too bright smile at Grimes.

"I guess so," he grumbled.

"Don't spend all your money in the same shop," advised the official. "And if it's dollies you want remember that you can have them made exactly to your specifications, while you wait, in the factory . . ."

He sauntered away.

Back in the camperfly Fenella got out a large shopping bag. Into it Grimes put the coveralls, the hard hats, the clipboards and the wire cutters. There was also a Vulcan Island street map which he folded and tucked into his pocket. They left their aircraft with Grimes carrying the bag, trying to make it appear that it was empty. There was transport from the airport to Vulcan City, a subway system. After the all-pervading drabness at ground level the brightly coloured advertisements lining the escalator were a pleasant relief.

There was colour, too, in Vulcan City but it was shabby, tawdry by daylight. The main street was busy enough however, with off duty shift workers staggering, so it seemed, from bar to bar. Grimes and Fenella Pruin looked into one of these, an establishment calling itself The Pink Pussy Cat. To raucous music a girl was dancing on the bar. She was not a very good dancer and her figure should have been decently concealed. Obviously she was a reject from one of the mainland places of entertainment. Grimes briefly wondered how long it would be before—what was her name?—before Tanya finished up here.

There were shops, some of which had window displays of ingenious mechanical toys, little dolls that stripped in time to the tinkling melodies from the music boxes on the polished tops of which they danced, other dolls that fled before horrendous monsters that snatched their clothing from them as they ran round and around their circular tracks. The sort of toys, thought Grimes, that one would buy as presents for kinky parents, never for well-brought-up children . . .

Fenella Pruin looked at her watch. "I hate to interrupt your perverted windowshopping, Grimes, but isn't it time that we were getting to the spaceport? It's almost 1400 now and *Willy Willy*'s due in just over an hour."

He put down the shopping bag, consulted the street map. It was not far from where they were now to the spaceport perimeter. The way was through a heavily industrialised area in which pedestrians, especially pedestrians dressed for leisure and pleasure, would be conspicuous. Fortunately there was a comfort station not far from where they were standing and even more fortunately it was not being used by anybody but themselves. Fenella took the shopping bag into one of the cubicles while Grimes studied the advertising matter decorating an aphrodisiac dispenser. After a minute or so she emerged, looking, in coveralls and hard hat, like a very ordinary female technician. Luckily she had thought to leave the camperfly wearing plain shoes rather than the golden sandals that she usually affected.

Grimes took the bag, retired to a cubicle. It did not take him long to change.

They walked briskly away from the city, along a wide street on either side of which were the drab grey walls of factories. Occasional heavy trucks, proceeding in both directions, passed them. The few people on foot were attired as they were. Nobody paid any attention to them although Grimes wished that the shopping bag, a somewhat gaudy affair, looked a little less like what it actually was and more like a tool bag.

At the end of the long, straight road they came to a high, wire mesh fence. Through it they could see the spaceport control tower and the lofty hulls of two big freighters. To their left a high wall made direct contact with the fence but to their right was a narrow alley. They walked into this. It was, so far as Grimes could determine, just a ribbon of waste space; there were no indications that it had ever been used for any purpose.

Somebody might look into it, however. Fenella Pruin stood so that her body shielded Grimes from view while he busied himself with the wire cutters. He had little trouble in clipping a square panel out of the mesh, freeing three sides only. He bent it inwards, stooped and passed through. Fenella followed him. He forced it back into place; unless somebody looked at the fence closely this evidence of a break-in would never be noticed.

Close by their entry point was a sort of minor junkyard. There was a battered looking wardroom bar unit, complete with counter, bottle racks, sink and refrigerator. There were autochefs, one large and one small, that obviously would never cook another meal. There was a playmaster with its screen smashed in. There were engineroom bits and pieces, all showing signs of extreme wear, that Grimes could not identify. (But he was never an engineer.)

He put the wire cutters back into the shopping bag, took out the two clipboards. He satisfied himself that both he and the girl sported an array of styluses in the breast pockets of their coveralls. Then he hid the bag beneath the counter of the bar unit.

They walked slowly away from the dump, clipboards in hand, trying to look busy. Fenella Pruin was using a stylus to make marks on the topmost form on her board. They headed, but not too purposefully, towards the triangle of bright, scarlet beacons marking *Willy Willy*'s berth. They were joined briefly by a man dressed as they were, although his coveralls were yellow and not grey. He said cheerfully, "I suppose you're hopin' to get first look at Cap'n Dreeble's cargo . . ."

"As a matter of fact," Grimes told him, "we're checking the arrangements for the next shipment of bulk Scotch."

"No reason why you shouldn't admire the scenery while you're doing it. *I* never miss a *Willy Willy* landing. All those odd little bitches . . . But they've *got* something that our women haven't.''

"Indeed?" asked Fenella Pruin coldly.

The man looked at her and grinned. "Jealous, huh? *You* haven't got a pair of legs like *them* . . ."

Grimes and Fenella Pruin changed direction, heading towards one of the warehouses. The man continued on towards *Willy Willy*'s berth.

"You took a risk," said Fenella to Grimes.

"How?"

"How do you know that *he's* not involved in the import of bulk spirits?"

"Because stencilled on his back were the words PORT VULCAN ELECTRONIC MAINTENANCE DIVISION.

He looked up at the hazy sky.

He could hear *Willy Willy* now, the distant grumble of her inertial drive, but could not yet see her. The noise was growing louder. Yes, there she was . . . A high, gleaming speck in the soft, overhead blue. Aloysius Dreeble was coming in fast. When Grimes had last tangled with him, many years ago, he had been mate of Drongo Kane's *Southerly Buster* and a good shiphandler. There was no reason to suppose that now, as master, he had lost any of his skill.

His landing technique was one that Grimes had employed himself, a controlled fall and then application of vertical thrust at almost the last moment. It was spectacular but safe enough—so long as the inertial drive did not decide to go on the blink when urgently required.

Grimes could see *Willy Willy* clearly now.

She was a typical Epsilon Class tramp, one of those sturdy workhorses of the Interstellar Transport Commission frequently disposed of, when obsolescent, to private owners. She dropped like the proverbial stone towards her berth, only a little clear of the two bulk carriers. Suddenly the mutter of her inertial drive rose to a cacophonous roar and she slowed, drifting down the last few metres more like a huge balloon than an enormously heavy spaceship. As she touched, in the exact centre of the triangle marked by the beacons, her drive was cut. She rocked a little in the tripedal landing gear formed by her vanes and then was quiet and still.

Vehicles were making towards her and a large number of spaceport workers. Grimes and Fenella Pruin joined these;

had they not done so they would have formed a very conspicuous minority. The after airlock door opened and the ramp was extended. Up this walked the usual boarding party—Customs, Port Health, Immigration. At the foot of the ramp stood uniformed guards, tough-looking, khakiclad men and women, stunguns out and ready. Herded by crewmen the passengers disembarked.

They were women, naked women, with the same anatomical peculiarities as the girls who had been the quarries of the kangaroo hunt in Katy's Kathouse. Most of them allowed themselves to be pushed into the waiting vans without any show of resistance. Two of them, however, broke away. They bounded over the spaceport apron, their hands held pawlike over their small breasts, not running anywhere in particular but just running . . . This was what the crowd had been waiting for. At least three dozen men took up the chase, yapping like dogs. It was all very funny—if you happened to be a sadist with simple tastes.

The port officials, with *Willy Willy*'s captain, had come ashore to watch the fun. Grimes looked at Dreeble. He thought, not for the first time, how well some people match their names—or how well their names match them. He was as weedy as ever, his features were strong on nose but deficient in chin. A few strands of black hair were plastered over the pallid baldness of his head.

Grimes looked at Dreeble—and, quite by chance, Dreeble looked at Grimes. He broke off his conversation with the Port Captain. He said, incredulously, "You!"

Grimes said nothing.

"You. Grimes. I'd recognise those ugly ears of yours anywhere. What the hell are you doing here?"

"Is there any law that says that I must be elsewhere?" countered Grimes.

The officer in charge of the guard was taking interest.

He asked, "Do you know this man, Captain Dreeble?"

"I did, once."

"Well, *I* don't. You! Do you have a spaceport pass?"

"I must have left it in my other clothes," said Grimes, after making a show of searching his pockets.

"Yeah? Captain Dreeble, who is this man? Who is that with him?"

"Her I don't know. He's Grimes. When I tangled with him last he was a two and a half ringer in the Survey Service but I did hear that he'd been emptied out. But he's up to no good."

"I'll take them in," said the officer, raising his stungun. "Are you coming quietly?"

Grimes would have done but Fenella Pruin endeared herself to the authorities by throwing her clipboard at Aloysius Dreeble before making a break for it. Grimes, paralysed but not unconscious, heard the shout of joy, the chorus of yapping as the hunters were given another woman to chase.

They caught her at last.

Fourteen

━━━●◉●━━━

They were dragged into a small office in the spaceport's administration block. Grimes was groggy, hardly able to stand, after the stungun blast. Fenella Pruin had been roughed up considerably by her initial captors. She had been stripped and would have been raped had the guards not intervened in time. Many women would have been cowed, humiliated, on the verge of collapse. She was not. She stood there in the ripped clothing that she had been allowed to resume, almost literally spitting with fury.

She screamed at the fat man in civilian clothes sitting behind the big desk, "I'll sue! I'll make this lousy spaceport pay and pay and pay for what was done to me!"

The fat man raised his eyebrows and smiled. "You will sue? But you are a trespasser. As such you have no rights." He turned to the master of *Willy Willy*. "Captain Dreeble, do you know these people?"

"I know the man, Colonel Dietrich. He is John Grimes. The last time I met him he was captain of the Federation Survey Service's *Seeker*. This woman I don't know."

"And what are you doing here on New Venusberg, Mr. Grimes?"

Grimes found it hard to talk; he still had not regained full control of his faculties. At last he croaked, "I am ownermaster of *Little Sister*, at present berthed at Port Aphrodite."

"And you, Miss?"

"I am Captain Grimes' passenger. His charterer, rather. And people who can afford to charter spaceships are not to be trifled with. Especially not on this money-hungry mud ball!"

"Your name, please?"

"Prunella Fenn, a citizen of Bronsonia. Our ambassador here will be told of what has happened to me!"

"Bronsonia has no ambassador on New Venusberg, Miss Fenn. I doubt if such a minor colony has representation on any other world."

"The Federation High Commissioner represents us."

"And will the Federation High Commissioner bother his arse about a pair of trespassers? Trespassers, moreover, who went to the trouble of disguising themselves. Trespassers who did not enter the spaceport through the gate; the records have been scanned and nobody of your appearance was seen to enter. In any case you have no identity badges. A search of the perimeter fence has been initiated; we shall soon know how you did get in."

"And much good will it do you!" sneered Fenella Pruin.

"And much good it will do *you*," replied the colonel mildly. He picked up an elongated sheet of paper that had been protruded through a slot in the surface of his desk. "Ah, the print-out from Port Aphrodite . . . You get quite a write-up, Captain Grimes. Always getting into trouble in the Survey Service, finally resigning after the *Discovery* mutiny. Yachtmaster for the Baroness d'Estang. Ownermaster of *Little Sister*, which used to be the deep space pinnace carried by the Baroness's Yacht. Quite an expensive little ship, your *Little Sister*. It says here that she's constructed from an isotope of gold . . . You should have no trouble in paying your fine . . .

"And now, Miss Fenn . . . Winner of the Bronson Bonanza Lottery. Blowing your winnings on a galactic tour, with first stop New Venusberg . . .

"But why, *why*, WHY should you and Grimes be trespassing on the Port Vulcan landing field?"

Aloysius Dreeble was looking hard at Fenella Pruin. He said, "I think that I may have the answer, Colonel. May I use your telephone?"

"Of course, Captain."

"What number has been allocated to my ship?"

"Seven six three," volunteered one of the uniformed officers.

Dreeble went to the colonel's desk, punched the number on the panel of the handset, picked up the instrument. "*Willy Willy*? Captain here. Get me the Chief Officer, please." There was a short delay. "Oh, Mr Pelkin . . . Will you go up to my day cabin and look in my bookcase . . . You'll find a bundle of old copies of *Star Scandals*, you know, that magazine they put out on New Maine . . . Will you bring them across to Colonel Dietrich's office?"

"Star Scandals?" murmured the colonel thoughtfully.

"Star Scandals!" said Fenella Pruin scornfully. "Does somebody here have some take-away food to wrap up?"

"Only crumpet," leered Dreeble.

She glared at him.

"You always seem to be getting into trouble, Captain Grimes, don't you," said the colonel, making conversation. "Weren't you involved in that *Bronson Star* affair?"

"Bronson Star . . ." repeated Dreeble. "Of course. Syndication . . ."

"I demand that we be released, with apologies!" snapped Fenella Pruin. "Are we to be held here while this disreputable tramp skipper paws through his cheap pornography?"

"There are writers as well as readers!" retorted Dreeble. "And some publications are more disreputable than any tramp ship could ever be!"

Dreeble's mate, a chubby, sullen young man, came in.

He said to his captain, "Your reading matter, sir."

"Put it on the colonel's desk, Mr Pelkin."

The spaceman dropped the bundle of gaudily covered magazines on to the polished surface. Dreeble started to sort through them.

"Ah, here we are! *Sex Slaves of Salacia*. By Fenella Pruin. Syndicated from *The Bronson Star* . . . And there's a picture of the distinguished authoress, Colonel."

Dietrich looked from the photograph to Fenella Pruin, then back again. "There *is* a resemblance . . ." he murmured. "And Fenella Pruin's from Bronsonia, as is Prunella Fenn . . ."

"I always read Fenella Pruin's pieces," said Dreeble. "In fact I am—or was—quite an admirer of hers. She's been in jail at least once, you know. I remember the article she did on the experience. *I Was A Prisoner Of The Prince Of Potsdam*. Kinky that prince was. Very kinky. Potsdam's one of the Waldegren planets, you know."

"I know," said Dietrich. "I've relatives living there."

"They'll have records on Potsdam, colonel. Fingerprints, retinal patterns, bone structure, the lot. Unless Miss Pruin—or her employers—went to the expense of a complete body sculpture job something is bound to match."

"If Miss Fenn *is* Miss Pruin," said Dietrich.

"Which of course, I am not," said that lady. "You'd better release us before you make further fools of yourselves."

"Captain Dreeble," said Grimes, sufficiently recovered to shove his oar in, "would be pleased and flattered to have as a passenger his favourite author. Do you think that I'd charter *my* ship to such a notorious woman?"

"You'd do anything for money, Grimes," said Dreeble. "For all your airs and graces you're no better than Drongo Kane or myself. What sort of rake-off did you get from the

Dog Star Line for interfering with our quite legitimate enterprises on Morrowvia?''

"You should know that officers of the Federation Survey
Service don't take rake-offs, Dreeble.''

"And is that why you're not in the Service now?''

"Gentlemen, gentlemen,'' admonished Dietrich. "This is
my office, not a spaceman's bar.'' He turned to a woman
officer. "Take Miss Fenn—or Miss Pruin—away and record
all, and I mean *all*, her personal data.'' Then, to one of his
male assistants. "Send a Carlottigram to the governor of the
Leipzig Jail on New Potsdam, over my name, requesting all
available information on Fenella Pruin . . .''

She tried to put up a struggle but stunguns flashed. She was
carried out.

"And now, Captain Grimes,'' said Dietrich, "I must invite
you to accept our hospitality until this little matter has been
cleared up.''

Grimes shrugged. A token resistance would do him no
good and would please only the obnoxious Dreeble. He let
himself be led out of the office and to a cell. This had a
heavily barred door, a hard bed, a water faucet, a drainage
hole in the corner for body wastes and a single overhead light
strip. It was not luxurious accommodation.

After he was locked in a guard pushed a bundle of magazines through the bars.

"With Captain Dreeble's compliments,'' he said, grinning.

Grimes wondered if Fenella Pruin would ever be writing
about the star scandal in which she and he were now involved.

Fifteen

—————•◦•—————

Inevitably Dreeble came to gloat.

He stood well back from the grille as though afraid that Grimes would reach out through the bars to grab his throat. He smirked greasily. He said, "You've had it, Grimes. You've really had it. It's a bloody pity that Drongo Kane's not here. He'd be enjoying this as much as I am."

Grimes said nothing.

"But I'm sorry about the Pruin bitch. She can really write, you know. I'll miss her pieces in Star Scandals and the other sexzines."

"So will plenty of others," said Grimes. "Including her employers back on Bronsonia. She's a valuable piece of property. But they know where she is. They'll soon buy her out of jail. They've done it before."

"I know. I've read her stories. But *The Bronson Star* will be told that she's missing, presumed dead, when they start making enquiries. It'll be a sad story. Shall I tell it to you?"

"Go ahead, if it amuses you."

"It's you that I want to amuse, Grimes. Well, she left Port Aphrodite in a hired camperfly. Correct? Piloted by yourself. And on a flight over the sea the thing just vanished. Pilot error? Pilot incompetence? Your guess is as good as mine."

Grimes laughed scornfully. "It's a known fact that we came in to the Vulcan Island airport. And the camperfly's still there."

"Is it?" Dreeble made an elaborate production of consulting his watch. "For your information, it should be lifting off about now. The good Colonel Dietrich has some talented people in his employ—masters of disguise and all that. So you and the fair Fenella, carrying your packaged purchases— lots of tourists do shopping in Vulcan City—will have boarded the camperfly. You have decided not to stay the night after all. You will tell Aerospace Control that you are bound for Delphi to consult the Oracle. (It's a pity that you didn't do that before you came here!)

"So you lift. So you wamble off to the west'ard. Out of sight of land a police launch will be waiting. By this time your impersonators will have unpacked their parcels. In two of them are minaturised, personal inertial drive units. The pseudo Grimes and the make-believe Fenella bail out, landing on the deck of the launch. The camperfly flies on. And that's where the third parcel comes in. Or goes off."

"A bomb?" asked Grimes.

"How did you guess? Anyhow, when you don't arrive at Delphi enquiries will be made and, eventually, a search initiated. A few shreds and splinters of wreckage may be found. But no Grimes. No Fenella Pruin. I imagine that she'll get quite nice obituaries in the rags she wrote for—but nobody is going to miss *you*."

"You missed your vocation, Dreeble," said Grimes. "You should have been a fiction writer. Do you really expect me to believe all this crap?"

"But you haven't heard the best of it yet, Grimes. As soon as your identities were established—the authorities on New Potsdam were very prompt and cooperative—the colonel made a full report to the New Venusberg committee of management. The Committee doesn't like snoopers. Too, most of its members are sadistic bastards. They decided that the punishment should fit the crime. You came here to find things out. Well, the pair of you are going to do just that. The hard way. My big regret is that Fenella Pruin will not survive to write about her experiences."

"If you're short of reading matter," Grimes told him, "you can always write your own. You'd be a good hand at pornographic fantasy."

"Fantasy, Grimes?"

"What else? This is a civilised planet. Decadent as all hell but still civilised. An Associate Member of the Interstellar Federation—and both Miss Pruin and I are citizens of the Federation. The only crime that we've committed is the minor one of trespass. I've no doubt that the very worst we can expect is a heavy fine followed by deportation.

"And Miss Pruin will get a story of sorts. There was that very nasty hunting down and gang rape of some of your passengers; I didn't notice *you* doing anything to protect them. I'll get my charter money. Oh, on your way out you might ask the colonel just how long he intends to keep me in this cell. I can afford bail, you know."

"Bail, Grimes? They might accept a pound of flesh, but

nothing less. You're in a jam, the very last jam of your
career, and don't forget it.''

"Fuck off, Dreeble," said Grimes tiredly. "Go and make
up some more sensational fiction."

"Isn't there a saying, Grimes, that truth is stranger than
fiction?'' retorted Dreeble as he walked away.

Sixteen

━━━━●━━━━

Grimes was fed at regular intervals—filling but savourless sludge. He was allowed toilet requisites—a towel, a washcloth, soap, depilatory cream. He was given a change of underclothing. But the guards who brought him these things refused to answer his questions, ignored his demands for an interview with Colonel Dietrich, a telephone call to the Federation High Commissioner. He could not find out what had happened to Fenella Pruin. Much as he disliked her he felt responsible for her. He realised that he was worrying more about her safety than his own.

And what if Dreeble's wild story were not fiction?

But it had to be.

Fenella Pruin was a famous journalist, known throughout the galaxy. He, as a shipmaster and a shipowner, was a person of some consequence and possessed some slight measure of fame himself. They couldn't just vanish. There would be enquiries made—and not only by people outside New Venusberg. Captain McKillick, for example. The Port Captain must already be wondering what had happened to his new inamorata . . .

But the faked camperfly disaster . . .

That would answer all questions, especially when identifiable wreckage was found.

And then one morning they came for Grimes. (He didn't know that it was morning until he was hustled out of the prison to a waiting van; his watch had been taken from him shortly after his arrest.) He was taken to the airport. The vehicle pulled up right alongside a big, inertial drive atmosphere transport; no bystander would be able to see who or what was transferred from car to aircraft. He was thrown into an unfurnished, padded cell, locked in.

Sitting there on the deck—it was comfortable enough—he could do nothing but wait and worry. Perhaps, he thought, he was just being given the bum's rush from Vulcan Island. Perhaps he was being taken back to Port Aphrodite where he

would be put aboard *Little Sister* and told to get off the planet
and never come back. As long as Fenella Pruin was with him
he would do just that, and thankfully.

He felt rather than heard—the padding of the cell was
effective sonic insulation—the aircraft coming to life. The
resilient material was depressed under the weight of his body
as the transport lifted. He sensed a turn, then forward motion.
He settled down to endure what he hoped would be only a
short voyage. He sorely missed his pipe but it, with other
possessions, had been confiscated. He was uncomfortably
aware of the fullness of his bladder. He looked in some
desperation around the cell. At last, by the dim illumination
of the overhead light, he found a panel in the deck covering
that lifted up and away. There was a drainhole under it.

Well, that was one pressing problem solved.

But there were others—many others.

He would cross these bridges when he came to them.

He drifted off into an uneasy sleep.

There was nothing else to do.

He woke up when the transport came in to a landing.

The door was flung open. Two burly, black uniformed
guards dragged him out into the alleyway; one of them snapped
handcuffs on to his wrists. He was pulled roughly to the open
door beyond which was the ramp, then on to the gangway.
He expected to see the familiar environs of Port Aphrodite but
he was disappointed. This was an airport of sorts, not a
spaceport, little more than a landing field in a valley ringed
by high, barren crags. The time was late evening. The sky
overhead was dark with a scattering of the brighter stars
already visible. The lights at ground level were sparse and
dim with an ominous ruddy quality.

Another small party was descending the gangway ahead of
Grimes and his captors. Another prisoner with two guards
. . . The back view of this person looked familiar.

"Fenella!" shouted Grimes.

She turned before the guards could restrain her. "Grimes!"
Then, "How many bloody times must I tell you that the
name, on this world, is Prunella Fenn?"

So she had retained her sense of humour.

"Shut up, you!" One of Grimes' escorts cuffed the side of
his head viciously. Then, to his companions further down the
ramp, "Get the Pruin bitch away from here, Pete, before she
can yap to her space chauffeur!"

"Grimes!" she yelled before she could be silenced, "have you got word to the High Commissioner?"

"No!" There was another blow, this time on the mouth. "No! Have you?"

She tried to reply but she was effectively silenced. Grimes had to stand there, in the grip of his guards, while she was dragged away, struggling, into the ominous dusk. He thought that she was taken to the lighted entrance of a tunnel. He assumed that he would be taken in the same direction but he was not, although it was also a tunnel into which he was pulled and prodded.

There was an underground railway with little, open cars running through dimly lit caverns. There was, at last, a platform beyond which were huge, steel doors that opened, but only enough to permit the ingress of one man, when one of the guards pressed a concealed button in the rock face. Grimes' handcuffs were unlocked and removed and he was literally thrown through the gap. He landed heavily on the rough floor, grazing his hands, tearing his clothing and skinning his knees. He scrambled to his feet, turned. The doorway had already closed.

He looked around. He was in a big chamber, more artificial than natural, like a ship's airlock on a gigantic scale. A door like the one through which he had been thrown was opening. So, he thought, he was supposed to pass through it. What was on the other side? Nothing pleasant, he was sure, but he would surely starve if he stayed here. Perhaps there would be food and water at the end of the rocky tunnel that was now revealed. Perhaps there would not be—but he had to find out.

He limped into the tunnel. The inner doors shut silently behind him. He was committed now. Under his thin-soled shoes the floor was smooth, possibly worn so by the passage of many feet, but the walls were rough. Light came from glowtubes set in the overhead.

Grimes sniffed. He could smell food. He listened. He could hear voices. He plodded on until he came to a right-angled bend. Beyond this the tunnel extended for only another thirty metres or so, then expanded into a huge cave. There were people there, many people, men and women, some clad in rags and some completely naked. Most of them were gathered around a long trough set against one of the walls. From this drifted savoury smelling steam. Grimes, followed his nose, joined the crowd. People, he saw, were dipping stone mugs into the stew. He wondered where he might obtain one of these utensils.

A big, shaggy-haired, heavily bearded man shouldered his way out of the mob. He was clad in the remains of some uniform; two gold bands gleamed on his surviving shoulder-board. Walking closely behind him were four women. Two of them, judging by the growths on head and body that were more like feline fur than human hair, were Morrowvians. The others, small-breasted and with heavy thighs and oddly jointed legs, could have been members of the same race as *Willy Willy*'s passengers.

The big man looked down at Grimes. "I haven't seen you before."

"I just got here," Grimes told him.

"You're a spacer, aren't you? You've got the look."

"Yes."

"So'm I. Second mate—or ex-second mate—of the not-so-good ship *Suchan*. And may the Odd Gods of the Galaxy rot Captain Bejlik's cotton socks. And his feet. And his knees. And his . . ."

"Where do I find a mug?" asked Grimes, eyeing and sniffing enviously the vessels held by the spaceman and his companions.

"Haven't they been feeding you?"

"Only prison mush. And the last time was some hours ago."

"We'll soon fix that. Darleen!" One of the heavy-haunched women stepped forward. "Give your pannikin to our friend here. You can soon find another one for yourself."

"I couldn't . . ." began Grimes.

"You will. This mayn't be Liberty Hall an' if you speak unkindly to *my* cats I'll knock your teeth in—but never let it be said that Jimmy O'Brien turned a deaf ear to the appeal of a fellow spaceman. The two of us are the only two spacers here now since Komatsu bought it . . . Are you any good with long range weapons, by the way? We need another expert for the team."

Grimes accepted the thick mug from the girl's hands. He could see chunks of meat and vegetables floating in the thick stew. It tasted as good as it looked and smelled.

After a satisfying gulp he said, "This is all very confusing, Mr. O'Brien . . ."

"Call me Jimmy."

"All right. Jimmy. But there are some things that I must

find out. First of all, has a woman called Prunella Fenn—or Fenella Pruin—been brought here?"

"No. You're the only newcomer we've had for days. Is she your girlfriend?"

"I'm responsible for her. Secondly, what *is* this place?"

"A barracks, you might call it."

"A slave barracks?"

"No. For gladiators."

For gladiators . . .

Grimes was not at all happy as he accompanied Jimmy O'Brien, the four women tailing along behind, across the floor of the huge cave. There was a lavish scattering of huge mattresses, most of which were occupied by groups of people eating and talking in low voices. Many of them turned to eye Grimes appraisingly as he walked slowly past.

"They're weighing you up," said O'Brien cheerfully. "They might be coming against you in the arena. They're wondering what you're good at." Then, "Here's our pad."

He motioned Grimes to sit down, then joined him. The four women waited until the men were comfortably settled before seating themselves.

O'Brien took a noisy gulp of stew then said, "Since it looks like you're one of us we'd better get to know each other. These . . ." he motioned towards the two Morrowvians, "are my pussies, Miala and Leeuni." (Miala's hair was white, in vivid contrast to her brown skin, while Leeuni's was tortoiseshell.) Keep your paws off them. And these, Darleen and Shirl, were Komatsu's girls." (They were horse-faced, but pleasantly so, and smiled at him diffidently.) "They're yours now. While you last. Or while they last.

"As I've already told you I am—or was—a spacer. My crime—if you call it that—was helping Miala to stow away aboard my ship. Miala's crime was stowing away. The Old Man—bad cess to him!—turned us in. Leeuni is a murderess—although the pimp she did in wasn't much loss.

"Shirl and Darleen were performers in some clipjoint called Katy's Kathouse. One of the so-called entertainments there is the kangaroo hunt. They were two of the kangaroos. The hunt finishes with the hunters raping the hunted. Well, the girls here didn't like being raped. Darleen kneed some fat slob of a tourist in the balls and Shirl just about bit the ear off another one. Katy—as far as she's concerned the customer is always right as long as he has a full wallet—took a very dim view.

"And now, what's your heartrending story? For a start, what do they call you?"

"My name is Grimes. John Grimes. I've a ship of my own—*Little Sister*. I'm on charter to *The Bronson Star*—it's a newspaper on a world called Bronsonia. I'm supposed to be looking after one of their star reporters—Fenella Pruin . . ."

"Fenella Pruin? I thought the name was familiar the first time you mentioned it. Doesn't she write for Star Scandals? And Grimes? Weren't you slung out of the Survey Service for mutiny?"

"I was mutinied against. And I resigned from the Service. Anyhow, Fenella Pruin hoped to uncover some interesting muck here. She and I were trespassing on the Vulcan Island spaceport to watch *Willy Willy* come in. The master, Aloysius Dreeble, recognised me and after we were arrested was also able to identify Fenella Pruin . . ."

"But do you come from New Alice, John Grimes?" asked one of the girls—Darleen, or Shirl? they could have been identical twins—in a puzzled voice with a peculiarly flat accent. "You talk like us."

"I'm Australian," said Grimes after a moment's thought.

"Australian! But Australia is where our ancestors came from!"

"Never mind old home week," said O'Brien. "Carry on, Grimes."

"That's all. They slung me in jail. I suppose that they did the same to Fenella Pruin. I saw her again, briefly, after the transport that brought us from Vulcan Island landed here. But she was taken somewhere before I could speak to her . . ."

"The Colosseum isn't the only attraction in these parts," said O'Brien slowly. "I've heard rumours—but only rumours—of something called the Snuff Palace . . ."

"But how do I get out of here? How do I find her?"

"You don't. That answers both questions. All you can hope to do is survive. It's not so bad being pitted against animals in the arena; you don't mind killing them so much to save yourself from being killed. But haven't you noticed how everybody here keeps themselves to themselves? There's a reason, a very good reason. We don't make friends outside our own teams. That was Komatsu's trouble. After he joined up with us he met a girl in one of the other groups, a woman of his own race. He got to know her. And then—I still think that it was intentional—our team was matched against hers. He was a long range fighter. She was too. When it came to the crunch he just stood there looking at her with that killing disc, a thing like a circular saw that you throw, in his hand. He just stood there. She was similarly armed and didn't hesitate. She threw her disc and just about took his head off. Then she snatched the short sword from her team leader and before he could stop her cut her own throat . . .''

"You mean this actually happened?" demanded Grimes.

"Of course it happened. Worse things happen here. But now—to business. You may be captain aboard your ship but I'm captain of this team. I'm one of the two short range fighters; my weapon's an axe. Darleen's the other one; she uses a club. Then Miala and Leeuni have long, sharp spears. Medium range, you might say. Shirl's long range—with a boomerang. I hope that you'll be able to make your contribution.''

"An arbalest," said Grimes. "Is that allowed?"

"An arbalest? What's that?"

"A crossbow."

"I've seen bows and arrows used here. There are probably crossbows in the armoury. *They* keep a stock of just about every weapon known to civilised—or uncivilised—man. If you ask for a broken bottle they'll give you one. But no firearms, of course. Even so—a crossbow . . . You really can use one?"

"Yes," said Grimes, hoping that the tuition had not worn off.

Then O'Brien said that it was time that he got some shuteye. He removed his ragged uniform, sprawled out on the mattress between the naked Miala and Leeuni. It became obvious that the three of them had no intention of going to sleep at once.

Grimes asked, rather embarrassedly, "Where do I go?"

"You will stay here," Darleen (or was it Shirl?) told him. "There is room on the pad for all of us."

"No, I means where do I go for . . . To wash and so on . . ."

"Come," said both girls as one.

They led him across the floor of the huge cave to a smaller one. In this were the toilet facilities, adequate in all respects save privacy. And those blasted girls refused to leave him and while he was enthroned, seated over the long trough through which rushed a stream of water, he was treated to the spectacle of two ladies who were more than just good friends taking a hot shower together. He wanted a shower himself; in the Vulcan jail he had been unable to enjoy anything better than cold sponge baths. He stripped, walked to one of the open stalls. Shirl (or was it Darleen?) accompanied him. The other New Alice girl took his discarded coveralls and underclothing to another stall to give them a much needed laundering.

He realised that in an odd sort of way he was enjoying himself. It was a long time since he had taken a shower with an attractive woman and much longer still since he had done so with one who washed him with such solicitude, working the spray of liquid detergent up to a soft lather with her gentle hands. He knew, as his own hands strayed, that she was his for the taking—but not here, not here. It was too public. Perhaps, if he survived, he would exhibit the same unconcern for an audience as those two lesbian ladies, as that heterosexual couple two shower stalls away.

And perhaps that trauma engendered by his horrid experiences aboard *Bronson Star* would be healed.

Just off the steam-filled ablutions cave there was a drying room in which a blast of hot air dried both their bodies and Grimes' clothing. To the girls' surprise and disappointment he resumed his garments. They took him back to the pad. O'Brien and his two women were sleeping soundly. It was not long before Grimes was following suit with Darleen on one side of him, Shirl on the other.

Seventeen

———◦◦◦———

Reveille was a vastly over-amplified trumpet call.

The gladiators—Grimes estimated their number to be about two hundred—were given time to make their morning toilet before another trumpet call announced breakfast. Ablutions facilities were adequate, there being more than one minor cavern for this purpose. Breakfast was stew again—but this time of fish, not meat. It was savoury enough.

"What happens now?" Grimes asked O'Brien.

"We just wait."

"Don't we get any time to practice with our weapons?"

"The only practice we get is in the arena. But when there's anybody new in a team—such as you—there are usually a few sort of breaking-in bouts against animals before you're pitted against fellow humans. Too, usually just one death is enough to satisfy the audience—although that depends a great deal on the supply of new gladiators." He laughed. "Most times it's a new member of a team who gets himself killed."

Cheerful bastard, thought Grimes.

"We'll look after you," said Shirl (or Darleen).

Grimes wished that he had pipe and tobacco to soothe his nerves. He looked around the cave. Nobody was smoking—and certainly there must be others like himself, craving the solace of nicotine. Perhaps this was part of the technique—a gladiator deprived of pipe, cigarettes or whatever must be a bad-tempered one. He said as much.

O'Brien laughed. "You should know by this time that smoking shortens the wind and all sorts of other horrid things. A non-smoking gladiator is a *fit* gladiator."

"Fit for what?" demanded Grimes.

"You want to survive, don't you?"

"I'd want to even more if I knew that there was some chance of getting out of here."

Again there was a deafening trumpet call, followed by a harsh voice. "Denton's team and Smith's team report to the armory! Denton's team and Smith's team report to the armory!"

Not far from O'Brien's pad a huge man got to his feet, followed by another smaller and more agile, followed by four slight women. Their faces were expressionless. They divested themselves of what little they were wearing, left the rags scattered on their mattress.

"Denton's a boxer," volunteered O'Brien. "He wears a horrid spiked affair on his arm called a *cestus*. The other fellow, Mallory, plays around with a net and trident. Two of the girls use lariats, the other two throw javelins. A nasty combination. I hope that we never come up against them . . ."

Denton, followed by his people, was walking slowly to the far end of the cave. His back was almost as hairy as the front of him. He slouched like some ungainly ape.

"And Smith?" asked Grimes, indicating the other team some distance away.

"Rapier, and his sidekick fancies himself with the sabre. The two medium range men use long spears and the two girls are archers. But not crossbows."

"And how long will the fight take?"

"We shall know when the survivors come back—unless they've all been taken to hospital. That happens quite often. Then we just have to wait for the next announcement."

"But why couldn't you—*we*—just refuse to go out and kill or be killed?"

"That's been tried," said O'Brien. "But it's not recommended. After just one warning the cave is flooded with a particularly nasty gas. It makes you vomit your guts up and feel as though you're being flayed alive. Needless to say the sit-down strikers aren't at all popular with the others . . ."

They sat on their big mattress and waited. All through the cave people were sitting on mattresses and waiting. Which team had drawn first blood? Was the crowd in a merciful mood? How many survivors would there be?

"I hope you're good with the arbalest," said O'Brien after a long silence.

"I've used one recently," said Grimes.

"At one of those fancy hunting camps, I suppose. Did you hit anything?"

"It wasn't at a hunting camp—but I did hit the target."

"What was it?"

"A Shaara blimp."

"A bloody big target," commented O'Brien glumly. "Anybody could hit anything that big as long as it was within range . . ." Then, "A Shaara blimp! You must have been fighting them. There'll be Shaara in the audience, you know. If any of us get injured it'll be thumbs down for sure.''

"Do you want me to resign from your team?" asked Grimes.

"It's too late now. *They* had you under full observation from the moment you entered the barracks. *They* know who was mug enough to take you under his wing.''

"And he's an Australian," put in either Darleen or Shirl. *"We* want him with us.''

"And shall I stand to attention while you all sing Waltzing Matilda?" asked O'Brien.

There was another long silence.

At last voices were heard from the far end of the cave. Grimes, with the others, turned to look. Denton had come back. He was limping badly. A deep slash on his face gleamed redly under the newly applied syntheskin. There was another gash on his right thigh. Two of his women followed him. They, too, had been wounded but not seriously enough to put them in hospital. And the other three team members?

"Dead . . ." Grimes heard Denton growl in answer to a question. "But we did for Smith and his bastards. All of them.''

The trumpet brayed.

Then—"O'Brien's team to the armory! O'Brien's team to the armory!"

"So it's only animals for us," muttered O'Brien. "I hope that they're nice, little, tame ones!"

"So do I," said Grimes.

"But they won't be," O'Brien told him.

Eighteen

————••◦•——————

O'Brien removed his rags of uniform, folding the clothing neatly before putting it down on the mattress.

"Get undressed," he ordered Grimes.

"Why?"

"It's the rule."

"We're issued with armour, I suppose?" asked Grimes as he shrugged out of his coveralls, assisted unnecessarily by Shirl and Darleen.

"Armour?" O'Brien laughed harshly. "Not on your sweet Nelly. The customers pay to see naked flesh, to see it torn and bleeding. But come on, all of you. Let's get the show on the road."

Following the big man they walked through the cave. Heads turned to follow their progress. Some expressions were sympathetic. Most said, all too clearly, *Thank the Odd Gods that it's not us. This time.*

There was a small, metal door in the rock wall which opened when they were almost up to it, which closed after them. They walked along a short tunnel, came to a brightly lit recess which, fantastically, seemed to be a shop, although the shopkeeper behind the wide counter was dressed as a Roman soldier, the only anachronisms in his attire being the wrist companion and the holstered stungun.

He smiled greasily at the gladiators.

"And what can I do you for today, Mr. O'Brien? Your usual battleaxe, I suppose? And for the ladies? Spears and boomerangs and a *nulla nulla?*" Behind him an assistant was taking the lethal tools down from racks. Grimes stared. There was indeed a remarkably comprehensive collection of weaponry. He was pleased to see that there were crossbows very similar to the ones that he had already used. "And for the new gentleman? I assume that he'll be wanting a long range weapon—unless you're changing the make-up of your team." He addressed Grimes directly. "We have a nice line in

100

shuriken, sir. There's been no demand for them since Mr.
Komatsu and Miss Tanaka—er—left us.''

"An arbalest," said Grimes. "And a dozen quarrels." He
added, "Please." To antagonise this fat slob, who would be
quite capable of issuing sub-standard weaponry, would be
foolish.

"An arbalest we can do you, sir. But not a dozen quarrels.
Two only is the rule. Of course, you can use them more than
once—if you can get them back, just as Miss Shirley can do
with her boomerangs . . .''

The assistant took an arbalest down from the rack, held it
up for Grimes' inspection.

"To your satisfaction, sir?" asked the pseudo-centurion.
"Good. Then let us not keep the customers waiting—*your*
customers, that is. Your props will be waiting for you in the
arena. And the best of luck, Mr. O'Brien. We shall be
watching on our trivi."

"Thank you," O'Brien said before moving on. Then, when
the party was out of earshot beyond a bend in the tunnel,
"That two-faced bastard! But we have to be polite to him . . .
My dream is to have him out on the sand against me one
day . . .''

They came to the last door. They stepped through it into
hot air, into dazzling sunlight reflected from white, freshly
raked sand. Trumpets blared martial music, accompanied by
drums and cymbals. There was some applause but it was
bored rather than enthusiastic.

Grimes, squinting against the harsh light, looked around
him. There were the tiers of canopied seats ringing the huge
arena. O'Brien's team, he thought, would not be playing
before a capacity house; nonetheless only about a third of the
seating was unoccupied. Some members of the audience were
dressed for the occasion in rather phoney looking togas and
gowns. There was a royal box under a very elaborate canopy,
the human occupants of which were clad in imperial purple.
The non-human ones were (but of course) Shaara.

"Our weapons," said O'Brien, walking towards where
these had been set down on the sand.

There was the wicked-looking battleaxe, the two long spears,
the steel arbalest with two short quarrels. There were a nobbly
wooden club and two boomerangs, but these cruciform and
not of the familiar crescent shape. *An arbalest and boomerangs*,
thought Grimes, *and that royal box within range* . . . But the

air shimmered above the fence dividing the lower tier of seats from the arena. It must be, he decided, a forcefield.

The music ceased.

An amplified voice announced, "And now, for our second event, Battler O'Brien and his team versus the sand rays of Sere! May the best beings win!"

O'Brien had picked up and was hefting the long-handled axe, the women had their own weapons in hand. Grimes loaded the arbalest. He wished that he had a pouch of some kind for the spare quarrel.

"Sand rays," muttered O'Brien. "Do you know them, Grimes? They skim over the surface, not quite flying. All teeth and leathery wings. There'll be six of the bastards. Aim for the single eye. Your crossbow will be better against 'em than Shirl's boomerangs . . ."

Would it be? Grimes wondered. Far too little effort had been required to cock the arbalest. It would not have anything like the range of the weapons that he had acquired at Camp Diana.

Again the trumpets brayed.

At the far end of the arena gates opened. In the darkness beyond them Grimes saw something stirring, a shadowy undulation. The gladiators waited tensely. "Try not to move," whispered O'Brien. "Movement attracts them." The audience waited impatiently. "Send Battler O'Brien in to chase them out!" screamed a woman. "He's just standing there doing nothing—and we're paying for it!"

"I'd like to send *you* in, you fat bitch!" O'Brien muttered.

The trumpets brayed again.

"You, O'Brien!" roared a voice from the speakers. "Jump up and down! Dance!"

"Get stuffed," O'Brien said. Probably he was heard; directional microphones must be trained on the team.

"O'Brien! Hear this! Unless you *do* something it's you and your people for the Snuff Palace—for one performance only!"

O'Brien brandished his battleaxe; the sunlight was reflected dazzlingly from the broad, polished blade. It was enough. The sandrays came out of the pen in line ahead, moving fast, the tips of their wings skimming the sand, throwing up a white, glittering spray. They were fearsome beasts, their huge, open mouths rimmed with long, sharp yellow teeth. In the centres of their domed heads balefully gleamed their single golden eyes.

Clear of the pen their formation opened up. Grimes se-

lected his target, took aim. The range, he thought, was still
too great but it was closing rapidly. Out of the corner of his
eye he saw Shirl throw her first boomerang but did not see
what result she achieved. At least she had not aimed at the
sand ray that he regarded as his . . . .

"Shoot!" O'Brien, was yelling. "Shoot, damn you!"

Grimes, before he pulled the trigger, elevated the arbalest
slightly. As he had suspected this was a relatively weak
weapon; the trajectory of the quarrel was far from flat. But
instinctively—or luckily—he had corrected accordingly. He
saw the bolt hit, stooped to fumble for the remaining one in
the sand. And then he had to reload.

By this time the sand rays—four of them—were among the
gladiators. A huge wing knocked Grimes sprawling. He heard
one of the girls scream, O'Brien roaring. He got to his feet,
still clutching the arbalest. Miala pushed him over as she
danced by, brandishing her long spear. Again he tried to get
up but Darleen was standing over him, legs astride. Her
heavy club smashed into the open mouth of a sand ray
coming in for the kill, splintering sword-like teeth but snatched
from her hand by those remaining. The huge, fast-moving
body swept her away from Grimes, passed over him in a
wave of evil smelling darkness. The long, barbed tail flicked
his chest, tearing the skin, drawing blood.

He got once again to his feet.

He ignored the melee over to his right; he got the impression that O'Brien, Miala and Leeuni were well able to take
care of themselves. He ran towards where the ray had the
struggling Darleen on the ground, worrying her like a terrier
with a rat. She was still alive, her long legs, all that could be
seen of her, were kicking frantically. Shirl was sprawled on
the back of the beast, her arms around the domed head, the
fingers of both eyes clawing at the single eye. The tail was
arching up, up, over and forward, its spiked tip stabbing
viciously down. Blood was running from the girl's back and
buttocks.

Grimes ran around to the front of the fight. He raised his
crossbow. At this range he could not miss. Shirl saw him,
withdrew her hands. He fired. The steel bolt drove through
the tough, glassy membrane protecting the eye, into the brain
beneath. The wings flailed in a brief flurry of sand and then
were still. Shirl joined Grimes to pull Darleen from under the
ray's head. Her body was a mass of blood, her own and the
green ichor from the animal's wounds.

But she could still grin up at them.

"I knocked most of the bastard's teeth out," she whispered, "but he could still give me a nasty suck . . ."

But what of the others?

The fight was almost over. Only one ray still survived and Miala and Leeuni were leaning on their long spears, watching O'Brien finish it off. Its tail was gone, and one wing. It was floundering around in a circle on the greenstained sand, whining almost supersonically. With a dazzling display of axemanship the big man was hacking off the other wing, piece by piece, working in from tip to root. The crowd, to judge from the applause, was loving the brutal spectacle.

It sickened Grimes.

He took the long spear from Leeuni's unresisting hand, awaited his chance and then drove the sharp point into the sand ray's eye.

The death flurry was both short and unspectacular. O'Brien lowered his axe, stood there glaring madly at Grimes.

He howled, "What did you do that for?"

"I was putting the beast out of its misery."

"You had no right. It was mine. Mine!"

Axe upraised again the maddened O'Brien charged at Grimes, who brought up the spear to defend himself. The blade of the weapon, still sharp, sheared off the head of the spear and, on the second swing lopped short the shaft with which he was trying to hold off his berserk assailant.

It was Darleen who saved Grimes' life. Or Shirl. Or both of them. A thin slab of sand ray's wing, flung by Shirl with force and accuracy, struck the descending blade of the axe, deflecting it. And Darleen, coming up behind O'Brien, hit him, hard, on the back of the head with her *nulla nulla*

He gasped, staggered.

Darleen hit him again.

He stumbled, sagged. He dropped the battleaxe then followed it to the sand. His hands made scrabbling motions.

The crowd was roaring, screaming. Grimes looked towards the royal box. A tall, portly man, wearing a purple toga and with something golden on his bald head, had both arms extended before him, was making a gesture that Grimes had no trouble in interpreting, with which he had no intention of complying.

Darleen, on the point of collapse herself but still holding her club, asked doubtfully, "Shall I?"

"No," said Grimes. *"No."*

The amplified voice came from the speakers, "Grimes! The verdict is thumbs down!"

"No!" he shouted defiantly.

"Darleen! Shirl! The verdict is thumbs down!"

"No!" they called.

Grimes heard movement behind him, turned to see the advancing guards in their archaic helmets and breastplates, their metallic kilts. Their pistols were modern enough.

Luckily they were only stunguns, Grimes thought as the blast hit him.

Before he lost consciousness he wondered if this were so lucky.

Nineteen

He woke up.

He heard screaming, thought fuzzily that he was still in the throes of some nightmare.

He opened his eyes, looked up at a low, white ceiling, featureless save for a light strip. He felt around himself with investigatory hands. He seemed to be on a resilient bed. He was alone.

But who was screaming?

He raised himself on his elbows, looked around. Before him was a blank white wall. To his right there was a similar view. To his left the wall was broken by an alcove in which were toilet facilities. But the noise—it had subsided now to a low whimpering—was coming from behind him. He drew up his knees, swung himself around on the bed and looked with sick horror at the fourth wall.

At first he thought that it was a window, one looking into an operating theatre. Then he realised that it was a big trivi screen. Under the too bright lights was a table, its white covering spattered with blood. Strapped to it, supine, spread-eagled, was a naked girl. Stooping over the table was a white-gowned, white capped, white masked surgeon. His gloves gleamed redly and wetly. A similarly clad woman stood a little back from him, holding a tray of glittering instruments. In the background were the tiers of seats with the avidly watching audience. Inevitably there were Shaara among them.

There was no anaesthetist.

The surgeon deepened and lengthened the abdominal incision, tossed the bloody scalpel back on to the instruments tray. He took from this retractors, used them to pull the lips of the horrible wound apart. There was a pattering of applause from the audience. Then, plunging his hands deep into the victim's body, he started to pull *things* out . . .

The screaming was dreadful.

Grimes just made it to the toilet alcove, vomited into the bowl. He stayed there, his hands clamped over his ears, shutting out most but not all of the noise. He heard, faintly, hand-clapping and cries of, "Encore! Encore!"

At last there was silence. He uncovered his ears and found that it was indeed so. He looked cautiously into the room. The big screen was blank, dead. He walked slowly towards it, fearing that it would come alive with some fresh scene of horror. He could find no controls; obviously it could not be turned off from this side. So his sadistic jailors, any time that they felt like it, could treat him to a preview of what might be his own eventual fate.

He wondered when they would be getting around to Shirl and Darleen. And himself. He wondered if they had already disposed of Fenella Pruin. She had not been the girl on the operating table; of that he was sure. He supposed glumly that he and the New Alice women would be given time to recover fully from the wounds that they had sustained in the arena; a torture victim who dies too soon deprives the spectators of the entertainment for which they have paid. He looked down at the transparent syntheskin dressing on his chest. The gash inflicted by the sand ray's tail seemed to be healing nicely. Too nicely.

Of course he could refuse to eat—when and if he got fed. (In spite of his recent nausea his belly was grumbling.) But what if he did? With modern techniques of compulsory feeding the hunger strike had long since ceased to be an effective protest weapon.

Out of the corner of his eye he saw a flicker of movement.

A hatch had opened at floor level and a tray had been pushed through on to the polished surface. The little door closed with an audible click. It fitted so perfectly that only a very close inspection of the wall revealed its existence.

But Grimes did not make this examination until later. He was more interested in the bowl, with a spoon beside it, sitting on the tray. Everything was made of what seemed to be compressed paper; there was nothing that could be used as a weapon, either against his jailors (if they ever showed themselves) or as an instrument for suicide.

The food, too—it was a thick stew—could well have been made of cardboard itself. But it seemed to be nourishing enough.

Unfortunately Grimes could not keep it down for long.

He was treated to an after dinner show—this time of a man being slowly roasted over a bed of glowing coals, embers that flared fitfully when fed by the drippings of fatty fluids.

Twenty

Time passed.

How much time Grimes did not know, although he did try to keep some track of it. He assumed that he was being fed at regular intervals, assumed, too, that he was being given three meals a day. The trays, bowls and spoons were made of a material that could be torn up and flushed away. He saved the spoons, laying out a row of them in the toilet alcove.

He tried to keep fit by exercising, by doing push-ups, situps and toe-touchings. He was far from sure that this was wise—the better the condition in which he maintained himself the longer it would take him to die under torture. But he could not abandon hope. Not for the first time in his life he thought that the immortal Mr Micawber must be among his ancestors. Something might—just might—turn up.

The worst feature of this period of incarceration was that he was beginning to look forward to the sadistic trivi shows. He tried to excuse himself by telling the censor in his mind that he watched so as to be assured that neither Fenella Pruin, Darleen or Shirl was one of the screaming victims. This was partly so—but he knew that he had, now and again in the past, enjoyed films in which were picturesque scenes of the maltreatment of naked women. These had only been make-believe sadism—or had they?—but this was the real thing.

It was when he became sexually stimulated that he really hated himself.

Then one night—if it was night—he was awakened by the notes of a bugle call, *reveille,* from the wall screen. (It made a change from the usual piercing screams.) He looked at the wall but there was no picture, only an ominous, ruddy glow.

A quite pleasant male voice said, "We have been observing you, Grimes."

"Surprise! Surprise!" he muttered sardonically.

"We have been observing you, Grimes," repeated the voice. "We have decided that you are promising raw material." (Grimes remembered a torture session that he had been unable to watch to a finish, that of a man being skinned alive.) "It may not surprise you to learn that many of our executioners are recruited from among the prisoners. You will be given the opportunity to join their number."

"Like hell I would!" almost shouted Grimes.

"The standard reaction," remarked the voice. "But you would be surprised to learn how many of our torturers have been recruited as you will be. After all, it boils down to a simple choice, that between being the killer or the killed. During your career in the Survey Service—and subsequently— that is a choice that you must have made, quite unconsciously, many and many a time. But when you made that choice in the past the death that you escaped would have been a relatively painless one. This time the death that you escape would have been extremely painful."

"The answer is NO!" shouted Grimes.

"Are you sure? As I have already said, we have watched you. We have observed that you were physically stimulated by many of the more picturesque punishments meted out to members of the opposite sex. You really hate women, Grimes, don't you? Soon, very soon, you will be given the opportunity to *do* something about it. And I warn you that if you fail to give satisfaction, if you refuse to take up the torturer's tools or if you accord the subjects the privilege of a too quick release, you will be given instruction in the techniques required for the infliction of a long-protracted passing—instruction from which you will not benefit as you will not survive it."

The red glow in the screen contracted to a single bright point, an evil star, then winked out.

And what would he do, Grimes asked himself, when it came to the crunch? What could he do? If failure to comply would mean only a quick death the choice would be a simple one—but he remembered vividly, too vividly, that wretch who had been skinned alive and that other one slowly roasting over the sizzling coals.

Then they came for him.

The four guards hustled him through what seemed like miles of corridors, cuffing him when he hesitated, prodding his naked back with the hard muzzles of their stunguns. They brought him into a large room, a sort of theatre in the round with the tiered seats already occupied by the audience. Over these the lighting was dim but Grimes could see men and women—and the inevitable Shaara. The stage was brightly lit by a single light sphere hanging above it. It was a set, and the other members of the cast were ready and waiting. there was a rack. There were two St. Andrew's crosses. There was a box, a sort of oven, glowing redly, from which protruded the wooden-handled ends of the hot irons. There was a table with an array of knives, large and small, straight and curved, gleaming evilly.

On the rack was Fenella Pruin. She looked at him. He looked at her. She was trying hard not to show her fear but it would have been impossible for one in her situation not to be hopelessly afraid. Strapped to one cross was Darleen, to the other was Shirl. Grimes remembered the show that he had watched with Fenella, the make-believe torturings of the women on the rack and the crucifixes. He remembered the fat man who had wanted to take her to see the real thing. He wondered if that swine were among these ghoulish spectators.

An amplified voice was speaking.

"Gentlebeings, the stars of the entertainment that we are about to witness are already known to each other. The man making his debut as an apprentice torturer is an offplanet spy who was apprehended by our security forces. He is being given the opportunity to redeem himself. The lady on the rack is his fellow agent. She will be punished for her crimes against society. The two ladies draped so attractively on their crosses abetted the man in his defiance of authority. Perhaps some of you were present on that occasion in the Colosseum. They will learn that it is unwise to transfer allegiances. Unfortunately for them it will be the last lesson of their lives . . ."

"Cut the cackle!" screamed Fenella Pruin defiantly.

"I would order you gagged," the unseen announcer went on, "but that would disappoint our customers, to whom shrieks and pitiful pleas for mercy are the universe's finest music.

"And now, Grimes, may I remind you that the show must go on? And soon, very soon. If there is too much hesitation on your part one of our experienced tormentors will usurp your star role and yours, although in an almost as important part, will be for one performance only.

"You see your working tools. The rack, the hot irons, the knives. You can use them in any order you please. Your original accomplice has stretched the truth so often that it would, perhaps, be an act of poetic justice if you stretched *her*. Or you might prefer to make a start on your more recent acquaintances, working on the principle of last in, first out. May I make a suggestion. Perhaps, during your early training in the use of various weapons, you became an expert knife thrower? And the young ladies come from a world whose inhabitants are experts in the use of thrown weapons . . . They would appreciate being despatched that way. But do not make it too fast, Grimes. You know what the consequences to you will be if you do. Just try to lop off an ear here, a nipple there. Aiming between their legs you could slice their labia quite painfully . . .''

Or I could use a knife on myself, thought Grimes. *But that wouldn't be any help to the women. Or I could kill one of them before the stunguns got me. But which one?*

Shirl was staring hard at him. She seemed to be trying to tell him something. She looked from him to the knives on the table, then up to the bright overhead light, screwing up her eyes exaggeratedly, then back to him. Grimes was no telepath but perhaps she was. Perhaps she was an unusually strong transmitter. There were glimmerings, only glimmerings, in his mind. Throwing weapons . . . Nocturnal vision, so often possessed by those of Terran but non-human ancestry, such as the Morrowvians . . . (He did not *know* what was the racial origin of the people of New Alice but he had his suspicions.)

There was a chance, he decided.

There was a chance for a quick death for the four of them—and a chance that they would not go to the grave unaccompanied.

But what of his own nocturnal vision? A sudden plunge into almost darkness would leave him as blind as the proverbial bat, and without the bat's sonar. But he had been trained to work in the dark, by feel, when necessary. As long as he had directions and distances fixed firmly in his mind . . .

"We are waiting, Grimes," said the voice. "Make up your mind. The choice is simple—torturer or torturee. And by being noble you won't help your lady friends. Perhaps a countdown will help you. Ten . . . Nine . . .''

Grimes walked slowly to the table, picked up a short knife in his left hand. Then he went to the electric brazier, pulled a hot iron out of the box. Its tip was incandescent.

"A knife *and* an iron . . .'' remarked the announcer. "This should be interesting. Which will he use first, I wonder? The knife, I imagine . . .''

Grimes moved to the centre of the stage. He was not quite directly beneath the overhead light, now (except for the ruddily glowing brazier) the only source of illumination in the theatre. And he was, he prayed to all the Odd Gods of the Galaxy, correctly sited for his next move.

Suddenly he threw the heavy iron upwards as hard as he could, transferring the knife to his right hand as soon as he had done so and running towards Shirl. The whirling, whitehot bar hit the glaring lamp, fortuitously the incandescent end first. Perhaps the plastic globe would not have broken had this not been so—but break it did.

There was darkness—complete insofar as Grimes and the members of the audience and the guards were concerned. Grimes had misjudged slightly, made heavy contact with Shirl's naked body a fraction of a second before he anticipated it. He heard the *ough* as the air was driven from her lungs. Both his hands went up to her left wrist, found the strap securing it to the arm of the cross. He slashed, felt the soft leather or plastic or whatever it was fall away. (That knife was *sharp*.) Then her right wrist . . . (At least one stungun was in operation now, to judge from the vicious buzzing, but the shooting was wild.) Then her right ankle. (She emitted a little scream as he inadvertently nicked her skin.) Then her left . . .

Freed from the cross she fell against him, then pushed away, saying, "Look after Darleen . . ."

He stumbled towards the other crucifix. He almost missed it, found it only by tripping over Darleen's right foot. Even though he fell he did not lose his hold on the knife. He scrambled to his feet, went to work on the girl's bonds. Meanwhile Shirl, to whom the glow from the brazier afforded adequate illumination, must have made her way to the table with the knives. There was no more buzzing of misaimed stunguns. There were shouts, screams. Somebody was yelling, "Lights! Lights!"

Darleen was released. Without a word she ran to join Shirl. Perhaps there were now no knives left to throw but there were still the hot irons and, in the arena she had preferred a club to throwing weapons . . .

But where was the rack? Where was Fenella Pruin? It was still too dark for anybody with normal eyesight to find his way around in the theatre and he had now lost all sense of direction.

"Fenella!" he shouted.

"Here!" Then, "Get a bloody move on!" she cried.

He stumbled in the direction from which her voice had

come. He found the rack the hard way, crashing into it, falling full length on to her nude body. She snapped irritably, "I want you to cut me loose, not make love to me!"

This time he had dropped the knife. He slid off her, down to the floor. He scrabbled around under the rack, to both sides of it. Then there was a brief flare of actinic light as one of Shirl's missiles hit some piece of electrical equipment, shorting it out. He saw the gleam of metal close by his groping hand. Just in time he was able to stop himself from picking it up by the blade.

As he cut through Fenella's bonds he realised that the theatre was now very quiet. All of the audience must either have escaped or been killed. (He did not think that they could have put up much of a fight.) Fenella pulled herself to her feet by holding on to his shoulders.

She asked, "What now?"

It was a good question, too good.

He said, after hesitation, "I kill you. Then the other two girls. Then myself."

"What!"

"Do you think that *they* will give us an easy death after all this?"

"So you want to die? *I* don't."

And neither did he, thought Grimes. But what chance of survival was there?

Yet the theatre should have been swarming with armed guards by now. It was not. Surely the show in which he, Fenella, Shirl and Darleen were the stars must have been monitored . . . Perhaps the monitoring was only a recording, with nobody watching it live . . . Perhaps the survivors of the massacre were still trying to find their way through the maze of tunnels and had not yet met anybody to whom to report that the actor and actresses had strayed from the script.

"Shirl! Darleen!" he called.

They came to him, their bodies palely luminous in the near-darkness.

"Some escaped," said Shirl. "We didn't get them all . . ."

"We have to escape ourselves. Find women about your build among the corpses. Strip them. Completely. Get dressed. And you, Fenella."

He found the body of a man. A thrown knife had penetrated his brain through his left eye, so there was not much blood. Grimes, hating the feel of the dead flesh, removed the shirt, the kilt, the underwear. At this latter he wrinkled his nose in disgust. He dressed in the shirt and kilt, found that the dead man's shoes fitted his feet.

Not far from him Fenella Pruin had taken the long dress off a tall, slim woman who no longer needed it, had put it on. She looked at him and said, "Let's go."

"Underwear," Grimes told her.

"But I can't wear that. She . . ."

"People usually do when they die. Take those panties off her and hide them under a seat. When the guards get here they'll find, among the other bodies, four completely naked ones. They'll think—for a short while—that they're us. I hope. Ready, all of you?"

"Ready!" said Shirl and Darleen.

"All right. Let's get out of here."

He led the way along an aisle. All the EXIT lights were out, of course, but surely an egress would not be hard to find. They passed through an opaquely panelled revolving door into a corridor that was, by comparison with the darkness of the theatre, brightly lit.

At the far end of this was a large group of men, running towards them.

Twenty-one

So the guards were on the way at last. How much did they know? Would it be possible, Grimes wondered, to bluff his way past them?

"Leave this to me . . ." whispered Fenella Pruin.

She ran towards the advancing party of armed men, staggering a little. (Her requisitioned sandals, Grimes learned later, were a size too small.) She yelled indignantly, "It took you long enough to get here!" Then, hysterically, "They're all dead in there! *Dead!* And what are *you* doing about it? I didn't pay good money to come here to be *murdered!* It's a *disgrace!* Vicious criminals allowed to run amuck with *weapons!* I'll sue!" She was screaming now. *"I'll sue!"*

The officer, a burly brute in grey leather, brass-studded shirt and kilt uniform raised a hand as though to dam the flood of angry words.

"Lady," he expostulated, "we have only just been told. By another lady who escaped . . ."

"Only just been told! What sort of supervision is there in this dump? Where do I find the manager?"

He ignored this question, asked one of his own.

"How many of them are there, and how armed?"

"With knives, iron bars, *anything*. There are four of them, a man and three women. Or there were . . ."

"There *were?*"

"When they got among us and started killing we managed to hide. Under the seats. And then . . . And then I peeped out and saw that they were fighting among themselves. Like wild beasts they were. So we made a break for it and ran . . ."

"I can't waste any more time on you, lady," said the officer brusquely. "I have to get in there to clear up the mess." He turned to Grimes. "Sir, will you accompany us? You might help to identify a few corpses."

"Not bloody likely!" sputtered Grimes indignantly. "It's *your* mess. You clear it up." He turned to the women. "Come, Angelica." (It was the first name that came into his

115

head.) ''And you two ladies. We will make our complaints to
the manager.''

"As you please, sir." He signalled to his men and led
them in a brisk trot to the theatre entrance.

Grimes and the women walked, not too fast, along the
corridor. They came to a cross passage, paused to take stock.
The women had been quick-witted enough to pick up hand-
bags although Grimes had not thought to tell them to do so.
His own kilt had come with attached sporran. In this he found
an almost empty notecase and another, much fatter, wallet
containing credit cards and other documentation. There was
also a passport. The late owner of all this had been a Wilburn
Callis, M.D., a native of Carinthia. Photograph and other
data did not match Grimes' personal specifications. Then,
most importantly, there was a card issued by the Colosseum
airport; the late Dr Callis, whose medical researches had
been so rudely interrupted, had flown here on his own—or
rented—wings.

Fenella Pruin, according to the contents of her handbag,
was Vera Slovnik, also from Carinthia. Like Dr Callis, Ms
Slovnik had preferred credit cards to folding money. Shirl
was Lisbeth McDonald from Rob Roy, one of the Waverley
planets, and Darleen was Eulalie Jones from Caribbea. As the
two New Alicians could almost have passed for twin sisters
this would prove awkward if, for any reason, a show of
passports were demanded.

Hastily restowing money and papers the party walked on.
Fortunately the corridor that they had taken was not a well-
frequented one; almost certainly the main thoroughfare to the
theatre from which they had escaped must now be extremely
busy, with guards, stretcher parties and, thought Grimes with
unkind satisfaction, the meat wagons.

They came to a large, illuminated wall map showing the
various levels. There was more than one theatre, Grimes saw.
The one from which they had escaped was the Grand Guignol.
Then there were the Living Barbecue, the Operating Theatre
and the Dungeon. But it was the airport that Grimes wanted.
It was not very far from where they now found themselves.
He memorised the directions and set off at a brisk walk, the
women following. A moving way carried them on the last
stage of their journey.

And then they were out into the cool night and Grimes,
having handed over the card, was paying the charges due
from the late Dr Callis' money. Relief at having escaped from

the horrors of the Snuff Palace was making him talkative. No, he told the attendant, he hadn't heard about the disturbance in the Grand Guignol. He and the ladies were checking out because, frankly, they found all this old-fashioned sadism rather boring, as a spectator sport. If members of the audience were allowed to participate—no, not as victims, ha, ha—it would be much more fun . . . So perhaps a spot of hunting at Camp Diana would be more entertaining . . . And the camperfly? Fuelled and provisioned? Thank you, thank you . . . (Money—not too much but just enough—changed hands.) And Aisle D, Number 7? Thank you, thank you . . .

They boarded the chubby aircraft and, with Grimes at the controls, lifted. He told Airport Control that the destination was Camp Diana.

Once they were up and clear Fenella Pruin turned on him and asked viciously, "Why did you have to run off at the mouth like that? It's a miracle that you didn't spill the beans!"

"I thought that it was in character . . ." said Grimes lamely.

"Whose character? *Yours?*"

"Leave him alone!" cried Darleen loyally. "He got us out of here, didn't he?"

"It was just his famous luck," snarled the Pruin. "Just hope and pray that it lasts."

Amen, thought Grimes. *A-bloody-men.*

Twenty-two

———•◉•———

There was a full set of charts aboard the camperfly, covering all of New Venusberg. There was electronic navigational equipment. There was an autopilot. It was a much bigger and far more luxurious aircraft than the one that Grimes had hired—how long ago?—at Port Aphrodite, one designed for use by tourists utterly lacking in airmanlike or navigational skills and to whom money would be no object.

Normally Grimes would have sneered at such a machine; he preferred to do things for himself rather than to have them done for him by robots. His contempt for push-button navigators was notorious. But now he would be content to leave things to the electronic intelligence while he got some much needed rest. It could be relied upon—he hoped—to steer a safe course over the seas, through the mountain passes, to Port Aphrodite. *Little Sister* must still be there. Once aboard her he and the women would be able to make their escape from this world of commercialised sex and sadism.

If his luck held.

For a while, however, he flew on manual control, on ostensible course for Camp Diana, until the camperfly was screened from sight of the Colosseum airport by the high hills. (On the chart the name Colosseum was not used; there was just an unnamed valley.) Then he switched to automatic and pushed the Port Aphrodite button, waited until he was sure that the aircraft had come around to the correct heading before going aft into the capacious cabin. Somebody, he saw, had been busy. There was a meal set out on the table—a tray of savoury pastries, a big pot of coffee, a bottle of brandy. Grimes looked and sniffed in anticipatory appreciation. Obviously the late Dr Callis had believed in doing himself well.

Darleen got up from her own seat, made a production of getting Grimes settled into a comfortable chair. Shirl poured him a mug of steaming coffee. Fenella Pruin watched sardonically.

"And now," she said, "perhaps the conquering hero will tell us what he intends doing next."

Grimes sipped his coffee, nibbled a pastry. He said. "I've set course for Port Aphrodite . . ."

"Straight back to your beloved *Little Sister,* of course."

"Do you have a sister, John?" asked Shirl. "You never told us."

"It's his ship," said Fenella.

The soft, background music, of which Grimes had hardly been conscious, was interrupted. "This is a news flash. A camperfly, number SCF2011, has been stolen from a private mountain resort in Caligula Valley. Its charterer, Dr Wilburn Callis, a visitor to New Venusberg, was murdered. Aboard the aircraft are two underpeople, females, and two true humans, a man and a woman. All four are dangerous criminals. Aircraft are requested to keep a sharp lookout for the stolen vehicle and to report any sighting at once.

"It is believed that the criminals will be heading towards Port Aphrodite."

The interrupted music resumed. Grimes gulped what was left of his coffee but his enjoyment of it had been ruined. Obviously the stolen camperfly was no longer an asset but a liability. He did not know what the aerial capability of the planetary police forces was but was certain that it must be considerable.

"Well," asked Fenella Pruin, "what are you going to do about it?"

He reached out for the box of Caribbean cigars, selected one of the slim, brown cylinders. It would not be as good as a pipe but he had long considered the fumes of smouldering tobacco an aid to thought. He ignited it with a flick of his fingernail, put the other end to his mouth. He inhaled. Shirl poured him more coffee.

"Aren't you going to *do* something?" demanded Fenella Pruin.

"I have no intention of flying into a screaming tizzy," he told her. "To begin with, I'm going to land. There may or may not be something flyable at the Colosseum that has the heels of us, but if there is it'll be after us as soon as they get it airborne . . ."

He got up from his chair, went forward to the control cab. He studied the screen which depicted the terrain over which they were flying, looked at the chart. But before he could bring the camperfly down he would have to get off the rhumb line—or was it a great circle course?—between the Colosseum and Port Aphrodite. There was enough metal in the camperfly's construction to make it a radar target, an anomalous echo that would be picked up by the instruments of pursuing aircraft.

He switched to manual, made a bold alteration of course to starboard. And was that a deep valley showing in the screen, ahead and a little to port? It was a dark rift of some kind, meandering through the general luminescence. He transferred his attention to the all-around lookout radar. The sky—ahead, astern, to both sides—was empty. So far. But he decided that it would be too big a risk to use landing lights.

At reduced speed he drifted down. The worst part of it was that the control cab was not designed for making a visual landing—not that much could be seen in the darkness. He watched the radar altimeter. Yes, that was a valley, or a canyon, and a deep one. He was directly over it now.

He stopped engines. The camperfly had sufficient buoyancy from its gas cells for its descent to be gentle. There was enough breeze, however, for it to be blown off its planned descent. Grimes restarted the engines to maneuver the unwieldy aircraft back into position, making allowance for leeway. But he could not foresee that at ground level there would be an eddy. The camperfly, instead of dropping neatly into the canyon, the walls of which gave ample clearance, drifted to the leeward rim. The port wing of the aircraft fouled something, crumpled. There was a loud hiss of escaping helium, audible even in the cabin. At first there was a violent lurch to starboard and then, as the damaged wing, no longer buoyant, tore free of the obstruction, a heeling over to port. On its side the camperfly dropped into the gulf. Luckily there was sufficient lift remaining in the undamaged gas cells for the descent to be a relatively gentle one.

She struck, with the port wing acting as a fender, cracking up beneath her. She settled, then almost at once was on the move again. Heavy blows shook her structure from beneath, from both sides. A strange, somehow fluid, roaring noise was audible in the control cab.

Grimes extricated himself from the tangle of female arms and legs into which he had been thrown, not as gently as he would have done in a situation of lesser urgency. He ignored the outraged squeals of the women. The dim lighting in the control cab was still on. He saw, through what had been the upper surface of the transparent dome and which was now a wall, this luminescence reflected from a black, swirling surface.

Water.

The camperfly had fallen into a swift running river and was being borne rapidly downstream. Even if she were holed by the rocks into which she was crashing there would be no danger of her sinking as long as the remaining gas cells remained intact. The situation, thought Grimes, could have been worse. This was better than either the Colosseum or the Snuff Palace.

Out of the frying pan, he thought, *and into the washing up water . . .*

Twenty-three

The women sorted themselves out, crawled aft into the main cabin. They reported that the camperfly did not seem to be making water. Shirl returned with cushions so that Grimes could make himself comfortable, Darleen brought him a bottle of brandy. He should, he knew, stay awake—but he had been through too much. If he forced himself to remain fully conscious for what remained of the night he would be in no fit state to cope with any emergencies that might arise. And he wanted Shirl and Darleen, who had already proven themselves, to be fighting fit when needed.

That left one obvious choice for a lookout.

"Fenella!" he called. "Come here, will you?"

"What for? What's wrong *now?* Are you going to make another of your marvelous landings?"

"Just come here!" shouted Grimes.

She came. It was too dark for Grimes to see her face but he knew that she was glaring at him. "Yes?" she demanded.

"I want you to stand the watch. Here. I'll be staying here myself. Wake me at once if anything happens."

"What about *them?* I'm paying for your services. They aren't."

"They're trained fighters. You aren't. I want them to get some sleep."

She capitulated suddenly.

"Oh, all right. I suppose you're right. Snore your bloody heads off, all three of you."

She plumped down beside Grimes, tried at first to avoid physical contact with him but the curvature of the surface on which they had disposed themselves made this impossible. She lit one of the late Dr Callis' cigars. Grimes inhaled her smoke hungrily. Nicotine might keep him awake for a little longer but was a price that he was prepared to pay.

"Did you bring any more of those things with you?" he asked.

"Yes. Want one?"

Grimes said that he did. He lit up.

She asked in a voice far removed from her usual bossiness, "Grimes, what's going to happen to us?"

He said, "I wish I knew. Or, perhaps, I'd rather not know . . ." The camperfly struck and bounced off a rock, throwing them closer together. "But we're still alive. And officially we're dead; that could be to our advantage. When we turn up, in person, singing and dancing, at Port Aphrodite that's going to throw a monkey-wrench into all sorts of machinery . . ."

"You said *when*, not *if* . . . And as for the singing and dancing, I'm going to sing. To high heaven. That's what I'm paid for—but I don't mind admitting that I often enjoy my work . . ." She drew on her cigar, exhaled slowly. "But I do wish that I'd be able to do something about these girls from New Alice . . ." She lowered her voice in case Shirl and Darleen should still be awake in the cabin, and listening. "But they're obviously underpeople. Some crazy Australian genetic engineer had kangaroo ova to play around with and produced his own idea of what humans should be. But they have no rights. As far as interstellar law's concerned they're nonhuman. Oh, I suppose I could try to get GSPCA interested, but . . ."

Grimes was dozing off. His cigar fell from his hand, was extinguished, with a sharp hiss, by the small amount of water that had entered the control cab. His head found a most agreeable nesting place between Fenella's head and shoulder. She made no attempt to dislodge it.

" . . . a slave trade's a slave trade whether or not the victims are strictly human . . ."

Dimly Grimes realized that somebody was snoring. It was himself.

" . . . the river seems to be getting wider . . ."

"Mphm . . ."

" . . . the . . ."

And that was the last that Grimes heard.

He was awakened by bright sunlight striking through the transparency of the control cab bubble. By his side Fenella Pruin was fast asleep, snoring gently. A duet of snores came from the cabin. He should have stayed on watch himself, he thought. Nobody in the party, however, would be any the worse for a good sleep.

From the bubble he could see ahead and astern and to port, but not to starboard. He could see the river bank, densely wooded and with high hills in the background. The scenery was not moving relatively to the camperfly—so, obviously, the camperfly was not moving relatively to the scenery. The bank was at least five hundred metres distant.

He extricated himself from the sleeping Fenella Pruin's embrace, clambered aft into the cabin. Shirl and Darleen were sprawled inelegantly on a pile of cushions and discarded clothing. They seemed to be all legs, all long, naked legs. Reluctantly Grimes looked away from them to what had been the starboard side of the cabin, to what was now the overhead. There was a door there. He could reach it, he thought, by clambering on the table which, bolted to the deck, was now on its side.

The table had only one leg. It was strong enough for normal loads but had not been designed to withstand shearing stresses. It broke. Grimes was thrown heavily on to the sleeping girls.

They snapped at once into full and vicious consciousness. Darleen's hands closed about his throat while Shirl's foot thudded heavily into his belly.

Then—"It's you," said Darleen, releasing him while Shirl checked her foot before it delivered a second blow.

Grimes rubbed the bruised skin of his neck.

"Yes. It's me. Can the pair of you lift me up to the door? There . . ."

They were quick on the uptake. Their strong arms went around him, hoisted him up. He was able to reach the catch of the door, slide it aft. They lifted him still further. He caught the rim of the opening, pulled himself up and through. He was standing just abaft the starboard wing. It must have acted as a sail; with wind was blowing across the river and had driven the camperfly on to a sandy beach. Beyond this there were trees and bushes, with feathery foliage, blue rather than green. There were hills in the not distant background. Darleen—she must have been lifted by Shirl—joined him.

She said, a little wistfully, "We could live here . . . There must be animals, and fruits, and nuts . . . And roots . . ."

"Mphm," grunted Grimes. Many years ago he had been obliged to live the simple life in Edenic circumstances and this was not among his most pleasant memories. "Mphm."

"Help me up!" came a voice from below.

Darleen fell supine to the surface on which she had been standing, lowered an arm through the aperture. Shirl's head appeared through the opening, then her shoulders, then her breasts, then all of her. She stood by Grimes, looking, as Darleen had looked, to what must have been to her a Promised Land.

"This is beaut," she said in a flat voice.

"Too right!" agreed Darleen, who was back on her feet.

"We could start a tribe," said Shirl.

Count me out as a patriarch, thought Grimes.

"Just the three of us," went on Shirl, "to start with . . ."

And did that mean the three women, Grimes wondered, or the two New Alicians only partnered by him, with Fenella Pruin somehow lost in the wash? The way that Shirl and Darleen were looking at him the answer to the question was obvious.

"This is just like the Murray Valley at home," said Darleen.

"Too right," agreed Shirl.

"But we can't stay here," said Grimes.

"Why not?" asked the two girls simultaneously.

"We have to get back to Port Aphrodite," he said.

"Why?" they countered.

Fenella Pruin's voice came from inside the camperfly. "Where is everybody? Grimes, where are you?"

"Here!" he called.

With some reluctance the two New Alicians helped her up to the side of the camperfly. Steadying herself with one hand on the up-pointing wing she looked around.

"All very pretty," she said at last, "but where are we?"

"Home," said Darleen.

"Home," said Shirl. "We will settle here—Darleen, John Grimes and myself. We will start a tribe . . ."

"You can stay if you like," said Darleen generously.

Fenella laughed. "I'm a big city girl," she said. "And, in any case, you'll have to ask the owners' permission before you set up house."

"The owners?" asked Grimes.

"Yes." She pointed. "The owners . . ."

They were coming down from between the trees and bushes, making their way to the beach. They were . . . human? Or humanoid.

Their arms were too short, their haunches too heavy. The women were almost breastless. Their skins were a dark, rich brown. Some of them carried long spears, some cruciform boomerangs, some heavy clubs.

They stared at the stranded camperfly, at Grimes and the three women.

"Good morning!" Grimes shouted.

"Gidday!" came an answering shout.

"Where are we?" he called.

"Kangaroo Valley!" came the reply.

Twenty-four

It had been a long day.

Grimes had supervised the stripping and dismantling of the camperfly, its breaking up into pieces that could be carried into the bush and hidden. Matilda's Children—as this tribe called itself—possessed some metal tools, saws, hammers and axes, and the construction of the aircraft was mainly of plastic. Nonetheless it had not been easy work.

And now it was late evening.

A fire was burning in the centre of the clearing, now little more than glowing coals. Over it, on a crude spit, the carcass of some animal, possibly a small deer, was roasting. The hot coals flared fitfully as melted fat and other juices fell on them. (Grimes remembered, all too vividly, some of the things that he had witnessed during his incarceration in the Snuff Palace. He did not think that he would want any meat when the meal was ready.) There were crude earthenware mugs of some brew that could almost have passed for beer. Grimes had no qualms regarding this.

"You're as safe here, cobber," said the grizzled Mal, who appeared to be the tribe's leader, "as anywhere else on this world. *They* don't bother us. They leave us be. An' we could use a bastard like you, with a bit o' mechanical knowhow. An' Shirl an' Darleen'll be good breedin' stock. They're young . . ." He looked over the rim of his mug at Fenella. "About you, lady, I ain't so certain . . ."

She laughed shortly. "And I ain't so certain about you, Mal. But could I have your story again? Everybody was so busy during the day that they couldn't find time to talk to me . . ."

"We're Matilda's Children," Mal told her. "We come from New Alice. We were brought here by a man called Drongo Kane who said that he was one of us, although he came from another planet. He promised us loads of lolly if we'd work on this world. An' there was loads of lolly, at first. An' then we, the first ones of us, started gettin' old. The

126

fat, rich bitches from all over, an' their husbands, wanted younger meat. Nobody wanted us any more. Not for *anything*. An' we had no skills apart from rogering. An' there was no way, no way at all, of gettin' back to where we belong . . .

"We were just turned loose . . .

"We found this valley. Over the years others of our people have joined us, some of them too old to work among the red lights any more, some of them escaped from places like the Colosseum. We get by."

"And why do you call this place Kangaroo Valley?" asked Fenella.

"It's a tradition, sort of. Whenever our people have lived together in a strange city, on a strange world, it's called Kangaroo Valley . . .

And there was a Kangaroo Valley in London, on Old Earth, thought Grimes. In a place called Earls Court. His father had told him about it when he was doing research on a historical novel the period of which was the Twentieth Century, Old Style. But the people living there had not been descended from kangaroos . . .

"But why Kangaroo Valley?" persisted Fenella. "What *is* a kangaroo?"

"An animal from our Dream Time," said Mal. "An animal that lived in Australia, on Earth, where our forefathers came from. On New Alice the kangaroo hunt is one of our traditional dances. It is performed here, for money, on New Venusberg."

"I've seen it," said Fenella.

"I've been it," said Shirl.

A humpy, a rough shelter of leaves and branches, had been allocated to Grimes and Fenella as their sleeping quarters. They retired to this after the feast. Grimes, unable to face the barbecued meat, had dined on rather flavourless but filling roots that had been roasted in the ashes. Fenella, in many ways tougher than he, had enjoyed the venison.

Settee cushions, salvaged from the camperfly, were their beds. They stretched out on these, each with a cigar from the aircraft's now much-depleted stock.

"Poor bastards," whispered Fenella. "Poor bastards, thinking themselves human when they're so obviously not. That reversion to their ancestral characteristics with age . . . In only a few years' time your precious Shirl and Darleen will look just like the older women. All that *they* lack is tails . . ."

"They're still victims of a white slave trade," said Grimes.

"Yes. But legally only animals. How do you think they started?"

"It must have been very similar to what happened on Morrowvia. One of the old guassjammers, driven off course by a magnetic storm, lost in Space and making a landing on the first world capable of supporting our kind of life . . . Probably a crash landing, with very few survivors, among them a genetic engineer . . . Fertilised kangaroo ova—but the Odd Gods of the Galazy alone know why!—in the ship's plasm bank . . ."

"Mankind," she said, "has made a habit of spreading its own favourite animals throughout the galaxy . . ."

"True. There are kangaroos on Botany Bay. Well, anyhow, the era of the gaussjammers was also the era of the underpeople. It got to the stage when the politicians, bowing to the pressure exerted by the trade unions, whose members found their livelihood being taken away by physically specialised underpeople, brought in legislation to make the manufacture of imitation human beings illegal. Of course, it was the imitation human beings themselves who were the main sufferers. And after all these many years the prejudice still persists . . ."

"Tell me," she asked, "have you ever conquered *your* prejudice against underpeople? In bed, I mean . . ."

"I don't think that I have any such prejudice."

"And did you and Shirl . . . Or Darleen . . .?"

"No," he said.

"The way that they look at you I thought that you and they must have been having it off. But you have this odd hang-up, don't you? You're afraid that when it's open and ready for you it's going to bite you . . ."

Yet her words did not wound, were not intended to do so. It was not what she was saying but the way that she was saying it that robbed them of their sting. The old Fenella Pruin—temporarily at least—was dead. This was a new one, engendered by the perils that they had faced together. The intimacy of this crude humpy was hardly greater than the intimacy of *Little Sister*'s living quarters, and yet . . .

He heard the rustle as she removed the dress that was her only clothing. He was not ready for her when she came to him but was aroused by the first kiss, by the feel of her body against his. She mounted him, rode him, rode him into the ground, reaching her climax as he reached his, as his body purged itself of the months of humiliations and frustrations.

She spoiled things—but only a little—when she murmured, "I got you before those two marsupial bitches did!"

But what would it be like, he wondered as he drifted into sleep, with Darleen?

Or Shirl?

Twenty-five

———•◉•———

Grimes expected that Fenella Pruin would be all sweetness and light the following morning. She was not. She started complaining almost as soon as she opened her eyes. To begin with it was the toilet facilities—a unisex trench latrine in the bushes, a cold bath in the billabong using a crude, home-made soap that would have been quite a good paint remover. Then it was breakfast—the remains of the previous night's feast, not even heated up, with only water to wash it down.

Then, puffing furiously at the last cigar, she led Grimes on a tour of inspection of the camp. She complained bitterly about the lack of a camera or other recording equipment and was more than a little inclined to blame Grimes for this deficiency. Grimes told her that she'd just have to make a thousand words worth one picture. She did not think that this was funny.

They were joined by Shirl and Darleen, who seemed to be in little better temper than Fenella. Shirl muttered, "They live rough, these people. Too rough . . ." Darleen said to her, "We should have got our paws on to some of those cushions . . ."

"There were plenty of cushions in the camperfly," said Grimes.

"And Mal's got them. Him and his wives," was the reply.

Fenella Pruin said something about male chauvinist pigs.

"Rank has its privileges," said Grimes.

She stalked on, stiff-legged, the others tailing after her. They came to what seemed to be an open air school. There were the children, squatting on the ground around their teachers. One of these, an elderly woman, was fashioning throwing spears, using a piece of broken glass to shape the ends of the straight sticks to a point. Another one, a man, was demonstrating how to make fire by friction, rubbing a pointed piece of hard wood up and down the groove in a softer piece that he held between his horny feet.

This teacher was Mal.

"Good morning," said Fenella, inplying by the tone of her voice that it wasn't.

Mal looked up. "Gidday. I'll find jobs for yer soon as I've finished with this mob."

Fenella ignored this offer. She asked. "These children . . . Were they born here? In Kangaroo Valley?"

"Most of 'em. But all born on this world."

"Were they all conceived here?" She was looking hard at one of the naked boys, who seemed to be in his early teens.

"Conceived?" asked Mal.

"Started. *You* know . . ."

"Oh. That. Some here. Some on the way here, from New Alice . . . Like Kev."

Grimes looked at Kev. There was something vaguely familiar about the youth's appearance. Physically he would not have attracted much attention on a bathing beach.

"And what ships did you come here in?" persisted Fenella Pruin.

"Just . . . ships."

"They must have had names."

"Yair. Lemme see, now. I came in one called Southerly something. *Southerly Buster*. Yair. That's it. Some o' the others in *Willy Willy*. An' *Bombora* . . . But yer wastin' my time an' it's time you did somethin' to earn yer own keep. What do yer do?"

"I'm doing it," she told him. "Now. I want to help you, Mal. You and your people . . ."

"You can help by bringin' in some firewood."

"You can help—yourself as well as us—by telling us how to get back to Port Aphrodite."

"You must be round the bend."

"I'm not. I have friends in Port Aphrodite. John Grimes has a ship there. Get us there and we'll be able to lift the lid off this planet."

"An' what good will it do *us?*"

"Plenty, I assure you. You'll be repatriated to your own world, if you so desire . . ."

"Rather stay here. I'm somebody here. A chief."

"But wouldn't you like to be recognised as such by the New Venusberg government? With rights, definite legal rights, for you and your people? Look at the money you could make from tourists, money that you could spend on little luxuries . . . Decent beer instead of the muck you brew yourselves from the Odd Gods of the Galaxy alone know what . . ."

"Nothin' wrong with *our* beer . . ."

But Mal, Grimes knew, had promptly commandeered the remaining bottles of Venuswasser from the wreck of the camperfly.

"An' there'll be women, Mal. Tourist women . . ."

"You're too skinny," he told her.

"Maybe I am. But before you were too old to perform in the house where you worked you must have enjoyed all the foreign pussy."

"I'm not too old!" he roared. "If you weren't such a bag o' bones I'd soon show yer! I was caught on the nest with the boss's wife—that's why I'm out here!"

"I never really thought that you were too old," said Fenella Pruin placatingly. She had moved so that she was between the morning sun and the chief, so that the strong light revealed the outlines of her body under the single, flimsy garment.

"Too bloody skinny," muttered Mal. "No bloody thanks!"

"Skinny perhaps," she said. "But rich certainly. Help us and I'll pay."

"What with?" he asked sceptically.

"I've money, plenty of money in the safe aboard Captain Grimes' ship."

"But it ain't here."

"I'll make out a promissory note . . ."

"There's only one thing that such a piece of paper would be any use for here."

"My word is good," she said. "And I have a name, a famous name . . ."

"Not to me it ain't."

Grimes was aware that Darleen was tugging at his sleeve. She had something to say to him, in private. He followed her into the bushes. Shirl accompanied them.

As soon as they were concealed from view, out of hearing from Mal and Fenella, she opened the shoulder bag that she was carrying, extracted a purse. It was very well filled, with notes of large denominations. So was the purse produced by Shirl. Evidently the dead women whose personal effects the New Alicians had appropriated had not believed in credit cards.

Grimes counted the money. It came to twelve thousand, three hundred and fifteen. Federation Credits.

"You take it," said Darleen. "On our world women do not handle business."

Grimes stuffed the notes into his sporran, walked back to where Mal and Fenella were still arguing.

"How much do you want to help us?" he asked bluntly.

Mal looked at him. "I was wonderin' why the hell you were lettin' this skinny bitch do all the dickerin'. How much have yer got?"

"How much do you want? A thousand?"

"Fifteen hundred. For you. But the tribe could do with three new women." He laughed nastily. "The ones we've got wear out pretty soon."

"The woman . . ." He corrected himself when he saw the way that Shirl and Darleen were looking at him. "The women come with me."

"That will cost yer, mister."

"Then an extra five hundred for each woman."

Mal spat. "Surely they're worth more to you than that. There's years o' wear in each of them."

"This is degrading!" flared Fenella Pruin.

"Isn't it?" agreed Grimes. "But keep out of this, will you?" Then, to Mal, "They aren't worth more than six hundred apiece."

"*She* ain't. All she's good for is collectin' firewood. But the other two sheilahs . . . Good breeders, by the looks of 'em. An' they're from my world. They're Matilda's Children, like me. So they'll be hunters. They'll be able to pull their weight."

"Six hundred for *her*, then . . ."

"You bastard!" snarled Fenella.

"Shut up! And a thousand each for the other two."

"Two thousand each."

Until now Grimes had been enjoying the chaffering. Now he was annoyed. "You mean," he demanded, "that they're worth more than me?"

"Too bloody right, mate. I need a spaceman in this camp like I need a hole in the head."

"Fifteen hundred each."

"No go. Two thousand. Cash on the nail and no bits of useless bumfodder."

Oh, well, thought Grimes, it wasn't *his* money. He said, "I have to talk this over, Mal."

"Don't take too long or I'll up the price."

Back in the bushes, with Fenella, Darleen and Shirl watching, he counted out the money. He had not wanted Mal to know how much was in his pouch. Six thousand, one hundred credits exactly; it was just as well that there was no need to ask Mal to make change.

The chief took the notes, made his own count.

"All right," he said. "You've sealed the bargain. You can loaf around all day, an' then ternight, when Cap'n Onslow comes by in his *Triton*, I'll get yer on board. He owes me a coupla favours."

Twenty-six

It had been too easy, thought Grimes. So far. He said as much to the women. Fenella said that it had been easy because he had been throwing money around like a drunken spaceman. Shirl said that Mal would not have been so keen to help had not two of his own people been involved. Fenella said that good money had been paid out but, at the moment there was only the vague promise of assistance. Darleen said that a New Alician's word was his bond. Fenella said, changing the subject slightly, that it was indeed strange that Mal was willing to get rid of his fellow Matilda's Children. Shirl said that the chief had set a far higher value on herself and Darleen than on Fenella.

Before the catfight got out of control Grimes steered the discussion on to what he hoped would be a safe track. He said, "The two of you were still yapping around the fire after Fenella and I turned in last night. What did you find out?"

"Kangaroo Valley ain't entirely cut off from the world," said Darleen. "It's left alone because it's useful. There's a sorta lizard livin' in rocky places. It ain't good eatin'—but there's some demand for parts of its guts. Haveter be dried in the sun, then roasted, then ground into a sorta powder . . . It sells at fancy prices in the cities . . ."

"What's it used for?" asked Grimes stupidly.

"What would anything be used for on this world? Mal doesn't sell it all, o' course. He keeps some for his own use. For all his big talk he's gettin' old, over the hill. He wanted us, last night. Both of us. An' he knew that he could only manage one with the amount of juice that he has in his batteries at his age. So he charged himself up . . ."

"An' the worst of it was," said Shirl, "that after he was quite finished he wouldn't let us sleep on the cushions in his humpy but bundled us off to get what rest we could on a bed o' leaves . . ."

"He's a jealous bastard, that Mal," went on Darleen. "He thought that you'd been havin' it off with us an' didn't want

you bustin' in and interferin'. But if the stuff is mixed in
drink—like beer—an' if the mug is shared by two people—
like you an' Fenella did once last night—it's supposed to
work for that couple only . . ."

Grimes looked at Fenella.

She looked at him.

She said coldly, "So that's why you were capable last
night."

He thought, *So that's why you weren't your usual bitchy
self.*

He said, "That stuff must be pricey."

"Even wholesale it's not all that cheap," she agreed.

"Then why is this camp so primitive?"

"Mal likes it that way. Matilda's Children like it that
way."

"What happens to the money?" persisted Grimes.

"It's banked. It builds up. Then, every year, there's a
lottery. The winner gets a passage back home, to New Alice."

"And yet," said Fenella Pruin, "Able Enterprises never
seem to have any trouble in getting new recruits for the
brothels—and worse—of this planet. Surely those lucky win-
ners spread the word about how things really are on New
Venusberg . . ."

"I met one," said Shirl, "just before I came out here. The
lying bitch! New Venusberg, according to her, was the original get-rich-quick-in-luxury planet. Ha!"

"Do you think that she was in Drongo Kane's pay?" asked
Grimes.

"Not necessarily," said Fenella Pruin. "A thorough brain-
scrubbing, then artificial memories . . ."

"But that's not legal," said Grimes.

"Some of the things that happened to us weren't legal. But
they happened just the same. The only crime here is not
having enough money to be able to break interstellar law with
impunity. So . . . But what else did you two find out during
your night of unbridled passion?"

Shirl and Darleen gave her almost identical dirty looks.

"Mal didn't want us for talking to," said Shirl. "But after
he threw us out we slept in a big humpy with two of his
wives. They wanted to spend what was left of the night
nattering. They told us what a hard life it was catchin' the
lizards, an' gutting 'em an' all the rest of it, an' how the only
thing to look forward to was Cap'n Onslow comin' in to
collect the . . . the . . ."

"Aphrodisiac," supplied Fenella.

"Yair. He always brings some decent beer an' some tins o' food, luxury items, like. He's from some world where the people have a thing about ships—the sort of ships that sail on the sea, I mean . . ."

"Atlantia?" asked Grimes. "Aquarius?"

"Aquarius. I think. He was a shipowner there, an' a captain. He sold out, came here for a holiday. He decided to stay after he found out that a little ship, with no crew to pay, could make a living sniffing around little settlements like this, pickin' up little parcels of cargo . . ."

"Sounds like a good life," said Grimes.

"You should know," said Fenella. "But perhaps he doesn't have the same uncanny genius for getting into trouble that you have."

"From here," Shirl went on, "he sails direct for Troy— that's a seaport just south of New Bali Beach. It's not all that far from Port Aphrodite."

"And then it's only a short tube ride back to my own ship," said Grimes.

"You hope," said Fenella Pruin. "We all hope. But first of all we must hope that this Onslow person will agree to carry us to Troy."

Twenty-seven

Late in the afternoon, just before sunset, *Triton* came up river. She was a smart little ship, gleaming white with a blue ribbon around her sleek hull. Her foredeck, abaft the raised fo'c's'le, was one long hatch served by two cranes, one forward and one aft. Her high poop seemed to be mainly accommodation. Atop the wheel house were antennae and the radar scanner, also a stubby mast from which flew Captain Onslow's houseflag, a golden trident on a sea-green ground. From the ensign staff fluttered the New Venusberg banner—the *crux ansata*, in gold, on crimson.

Grimes expected that she would be anchoring in the stream as Kangaroo Valley was devoid of wharfage. But she did not. With helm hard over she turned smartly through ninety degrees, ran up on to the beach. She moved smoothly over the sand until only the extremity of her stern was in the water. Then she stopped. From the port side of her poop a treaded ramp extended itself, the lower end of this resting on the ground.

There was movement in *Triton*'s wheelhouse as whoever was there left the control position. Shortly afterwards a short, solidly built man appeared at the head of the gangway, walked decisively down it. He was bare-footed and clad, somewhat incongruously, in a garishly patterned sarong and a uniform cap, the peak of which was lavishly gold-encrusted. He was brown-skinned, red-bearded.

He greeted Mal, who was standing there to meet him, "Hello, you old marsupial bastard! How yer goin'?"

"I am not a marsupial, Cap'n Onslow," said Mal stiffly, obviously not for the first time.

"There're marsupials in yer family tree, Mal . . ."

"Kangaroos don't climb, Cap'n."

Then what was an old-established ritual was broken. Onslow stared at Fenella who, with Grimes and Darleen and Shirl, was standing a little apart from the villagers. She was clothed, while all the other women were naked—but even if she had not been her differences from them would have been obvious.

138

"Hello, hello," said Onslow slowly, "who's *this?*" Then, "Don't I know you, lady?"

"You may have seen my photograph, Captain," Fenella told him.

"M'm. Yes. Could be. But where?"

Another Faithful Reader, thought Grimes.

"Star Scandals," she said.

"And what's a nice girl like you doing in a place like this?" asked Onslow with a leer.

"Getting a story," she said.

"Ah!" exclaimed the seaman. "Got it! Fenella Pruin! I like your stuff. This is an honour, meeting you."

Mal interrupted. "Cap'n, we have business . . ."

"You mean that you want some cold beer, you old bastard. All right, come on board." He turned back to Fenella. "I'll see you later, Miz Pruin."

He led the chief to the gangway, then up into *Triton*'s accommodation block.

"Why did you have to tell him your name?" Grimes demanded.

"I could see that he recognised me. It cost me nothing to be nice to him, to get him on our side from the start."

"Dreeble recognised you—and look where that got us!"

"He recognised *you* first, and that was the start of our troubles."

Onslow had come back to the head of his gangway, was calling out, "Miz Pruin, will you come on board? And bring him with you."

Grimes didn't much like being referred to as "him" and, to judge from their expressions, Darleen and Shirl resented being excluded from the invitation. They looked after him reproachfully as he walked with Fenella across the firm sand, followed her up the ramp.

Onslow—he was still wearing his cap with the ornate badge and the huge helping of scrambled egg—threw the girl a flamboyant salute as she reached the deck. He took her elbow with a meaty hand to guide her through a doorway into the accommodation. He had to relinquish his grip when they came to the companionway; it was too narrow for two to walk abreast. He went up first. Fenella followed. Grimes followed her.

As they climbed to the captain's quarters Grimes looked about curiously. They passed a little galley with an autochef that would not have looked out of place aboard a spaceship.

There was a deck which was occupied by what seemed to be passenger cabins. Finally, directly below the wheelhouse-chartroom, was Captain Onslow's suite. There was a large sitting room with bedroom and bathroom opening off it. In the sitting room, sprawling in one of the pneumatic chairs, Mal was drinking beer from a can bedewed with condensation. Three empty cans were on the deck beside him.

Onslow ushered Fenella into another pneumatic chair, took a seat himself. Grimes sat down in another of the modified bladders; he had not been invited to do so but saw no reason to remain standing. The captain reached out to the low table for a can of beer, opened it and handed it to Fenella. He took one for himself. Mal helped himself to another one.

"May I?" asked Grimes, extending his hand to the table.

"Go ahead. This is Liberty Hall; you can piss out of the window and put my only sister in the family way."

"Don't you have a ship's cat, Captain?" asked Grimes.

"No. But what's it to you?"

"He's just being awkward," said Fenella Pruin. "He's good at that."

"He looks the type," agreed Onslow. "Now, Miz Pruin, Mal tells me that you're in some kind of trouble, that you want to get back to Port Aphrodite without using the more usual means of public transport. As you've noticed, I have passenger accommodation. I understand that you require passage for yourself, for the two New Alice girls who're with you and for Mr . . . Mr . . .?"

"Grimes," said the owner of that name. "Captain Grimes."

"Captain, eh? Spacer, aren't you? Must be. I know all the seamen on this planet. There aren't all that many of us." His manner towards Grimes was now more affable. "What's your ship?"

"*Little Sister*," said Grimes.

"*Little Sister* . . . Captain Grimes . . . There was something about you in the news a while back . . . Now, what was it? Oh, yes. You and some wench called Prunella Fenn went missing on a flight from Vulcan Island to somewhere or other in a hired camperfly . . . *Prunella Fenn*" . . . He looked hard at Fenella and laughed. "I've read your stories in *Scandals*, Miz Pruin. How you've often had to sail under false colours to get them. But I never dreamed that I'd ever meet you while you were doing it—or meet you at all, come to that!

"And what will you be writing about New Venusberg? You don't have to dig very deep to turn up muck here. Will it be about Big Mal and his people? About how they got to Kangaroo Valley? About the lottery rip-off?''

"Possibly," she said. "You'll read it in *Star Scandals*. I doubt very much if that issue will be on sale here. I'll send you a copy."

"And will you autograph it for me?"

"I just might," she said.

"I'll be looking forward to it. But shall we get down to business? The cargo should be down to the beach by now; I want to get it loaded so that we can start the party. Now—passage for four aboard *Triton* . . ." He looked at Fenella. She looked at him. "Make that passages for three. You, Captain, and your two popsies. Three times fifteen hundred comes to four thousand, five hundred credits. Food provided, drinks extra."

"I thought," said Grimes, staring at Mal, "that we'd already paid."

"You paid," said the chief, "just for the . . . arranging . . ."

You money-grubbing bastard, thought Grimes, but without overmuch bitterness. Agents, after all, are entitled to their fees, although a mere 10% is the usual rake-off. He did mental arithmetic. He could afford the fares and have something left over for booze and tobacco. Fenella's drinks and smokes would be, he was quite certain, on the house.

"All right," he said to Onslow.

"Cash on the nail, Captain Grimes."

Grimes fumbled in his sporran, produced the money demanded.

He asked, as he handed it over, "Do we get tickets?"

"You don't. The First Galactic Bank still owns a large hunk of this ship—according to my reckoning it's from the fo'c's'le head to about the middle of the main hatch—and the less they know about what I make on the side the better. Thank you, Captain." He got up, put the money into a drawer in his desk. "Finish your beer, Mal. Let's get up top and see about loading your precious prick stiffener."

Grimes and Fenella accompanied Onslow and Mal up to the wheelhouse. Looking down on to the foredeck Grimes saw that a dozen Matilda's Children were already on board, waiting for the hatch to be opened. They were all women, as were the other stevedores standing around the big heap of bulging plastic bags on the sand just off *Triton*'s port side.

Onslow threw the cover off a console below the port
window of the wheelhouse. He touched a button and this
opened, the glass panel sliding downwards. He fingered another control and the forward deck crane came to life, the jib
lifting and slewing, coming to rest as soon as the captain was
satisfied that everything was in working order. A small lever
was flicked over and the hatch lids lifted, running almost
noiselessly to their stowage just abaft the fo'c's'le, leaving
the forward end of the hatchway open. A vertical ladder was
revealed just inside the coaming. Down this clambered the
Matilda's Children, looking like abnormally heavily rumped
naked apes.

The weighted crane hook dropped into the aperture, rose
after a short interval with a tray, on a double bridle, hanging
from it. This swung outboard, was lowered to the sand.
Working fast and efficiently the women on the beach loaded
it with a dozen plastic bags. It was lifted, swung inboard and
dropped swiftly into the hatch.

Grimes watched, fascinated by this combination of modern
automation with methods of cargo handling almost as old as
the sea-going ship. It seemed to be working all right. He said
as much.

"And why the hell shouldn't it?" demanded Onslow.
"Human beings—or, as in this case, their facsimiles—are
only machines. Non-specialised machines. On some worlds
they cost a damn' sight less than the sort o' machines that are
built out of metal and plastic. An' who the hell is going to
pay for roll-on-roll-off and containerisation facilities in little,
used-once-in-a-blue-moon ports like Kangaroo Valley?"

The stack of bags on the beach was fast diminishing as
Onslow played his crane with practised ease. The sun was
well down but it was not yet properly dark when the last tray
was brought on board. The stevedores came up the ladder,
their bodies glistening in the glare of the floodlights shining
down from the bridge superstructure, from the crane jib. The
hatch lids, like a pack of cards toppling, piece by piece, from
an on-edge position, ran back into their places, settled with an
audible *thunk*.

"That's that," said Onslow smugly. "Loading completed.
Now all I have to do is sail when I feel like it—which won't
be until not too bright and early tomorrow morning."

"Aren't you going to check the stowage, Captain?" asked
Grimes.

"Why should I? All that those bitches had to do was make

a single tier of bags over what was already there, cases of canned lemonfish from Port Poseidon . . ."

"Lemonfish is quite a delicacy, isn't it. What about pilferage?"

Onslow laughed. "With the stevedores stark naked? And they're *big* cans . . ." He lowered the jib of the crane into its crutch, switched off everything on the console, replaced the cover. He turned to Mal. "I'm ready for the party whether you are or not. Have some of your people come on board for the beer and all the rest of it. All this cargo handling has given me an appetite. And a thirst."

Twenty-eight

——◦◉◦——

It was a wet party.

It was too wet for Grimes, who was not in the mood for heavy drinking that night. It was too wet, presumably, for Fenella Pruin and Captain Onslow, who absented themselves before the orgy got properly under way. Mal vanished too, and with him both Shirl and Darleen. The fat lady who was plying Grimes with can after can of beer (now lukewarm) and who was trying to spoonfeed him with some sort of salty fishpaste straight from the tin was not at all to his taste.

He broke away from her at last. (It was like disentangling himself from the embraces of a hot-blooded octopus; surely she possessed more than the usual quota of arms and legs.) He walked a little unsteadily down the beach to *Triton*, the high-flaring bonfire behind him casting a shadow before that wavered even more than he himself was doing. Raucous shouts, screams and drunken laughter were unmusical in his ears.

Triton was in darkness save for the light at the head of the gangway and a single flood at the fore end of the bridge superstructure. Grimes climbed the treaded ramp. The door into the accommodation was closed. He had to stand there until the security scanner, which had been programmed by Captain Onslow to recognise his passengers, identified him. It took its time about it while Grimes, in growing discomfort, shifted from foot to foot. He had taken too much beer and, away from the fire, the night air was chilly. Finally a bell chimed softly and the door opened. He hurried up to the passenger deck, went first of all to the common bathroom. Then, feeling much lighter, he looked into the cabin that had been allocated to Fenella Pruin. She was not there, of course. Neither were Shirl and Darleen in their berths. He had not expected them to be. He conceded grudgingly that Mal and Onslow were entitled to their *droit de signeur*. He, himself, was entitled to nothing and would not be until he was back on board his own ship.

He turned in.

*   *   *

He was awakened by an odd grinding noise that came from somewhere below, sensation as much as sound. He was aware that the ship was moving. She must be sliding stern first down to the river on the rollers set into her flat keel. (That peculiar construction had seemed outrageous to him but it seemed to be working all right.) He slid out of his bunk, pulled on his kilt and shirt. (He should have washed the drip-dry garments before retiring; they were unpleasantly sticky on his skin.) He went into the alleyway. He looked briefly into Shirl's and Darleen's cabins. They were aboard. Shirl had her back to him. Darleen, sprawled on her back and snoring, looked very much the worse for wear.

He went up to the wheelhouse.

Onslow was there, in his inevitable rig of the day, sarong and uniform cap, busy at the manoeuvring console. Fenella, in a borrowed sarong, was standing beside him, sipping noisily from a big mug of coffee.

She turned to look at Grimes.

She said, "Stick around. You might learn something about shiphandling."

Grimes watched with interest. It all looked very simple. *Triton* had backed out into midstream and now was swinging to head down river. Onslow's big hands played over the controls like those of a master pianist. Then, satisfied, he made a last setting and stepped back.

He told his audience, "She'll look after herself now. Radar controlled steering'll keep her in mid-channel . . ."

"Shall we go down for breakfast, Clarrie?" asked Fenella.

"I'll be staying up here until we're over the bar. In narrow waters anything might happen." He turned to Grimes. "Can you handle an autochef, Captain? The one here is the standard spaceship pattern. You'll find eggs in the galley, and sliced bread, and ham . . . What about an omelet? And some more coffee?"

"Given an autochef to play with," said Fenella, "he kids himself that he's in the *cordon bleu* class."

"I'll manage," said Grimes. He would have preferred to stay in the wheelhouse to admire the passing scenery but he wanted breakfast. Obviously that was a meal which he would not enjoy unless he cooked it himself.

He went down to the galley. He found the eggs and the ham, broke a dozen of the former into the labelled funnel—

FLUIDS & SEMI-FLUIDS—and fed hunks of ham into another one—SOLIDS. On the keyboard he typed *Omelets—Ham—3. Execute.*

The autochef hummed happily to itself while Grimes poured a mug of hot, black coffee from the dispenser. He was still drinking it when the *Ready* gong sounded. He put the mug down and threw slices of bread into the toasting attachment. Almost immediately the gong sounded again.

Oh, well, thought Grimes, he would just have to finish his coffee on the bridge.

He found a big tray, and plates and eating irons. He took the omelets from the autochef. They looked and smelled good. He loaded the tray. He knew how Fenella liked her coffee; he guessed that Onslow would want his black and sweet.

He managed to get up the companionways to the wheelhouse without dropping or spilling anything. He had expected that he would be welcome, but he was not. Fenella was leaning out of a forward window; Onslow was close, very close, behind her. Grimes coughed tactfully.

Onslow stepped back from Fenella, adjusting his sarong. Hers was on the deck about her ankles. She stooped to pull it up about her slim body before she turned. She glared at Grimes while Onslow looked at him almost apologetically.

She snarled. "You took so bloody long that we . . ."

Onslow pulled up a folding table, said, "Just put the tray down here, will you?"

Grimes did so.

"Thank you," said Onslow. "Yes, we can manage three omelets, I think, between the two of us." Then, "Oh, by the way, Captain Grimes, I don't encourage passengers on my bridge, especially in pilotage waters."

So Fenella wasn't a passenger? thought Grimes. But she was working her passage, of course . . .

He left the wheelhouse, his prominent ears aflame.

On his way back to the galley he paused on the passenger deck. Shirl and Darleen were still sleeping, both of them snoring. So he would have to eat alone. This time he gave rather more thought to the preparation of the meal, using a tomato-like fruit and a sprinkling of herbs as well as ham for the filling of his omelet. He found a bottle of brandy and added a slug to his coffee.

He ate sitting on a small hatch on the little area of deck abaft the bridge superstructure, watching the scenery slide

past, the wooded banks the shallow bays with their golden
beaches. He was joined by Shirl (or Darleen; they had been
dressed differently on making their escape from the Snuff
Palace but now that they had reverted to nudity he had trouble
telling them apart) on the hatch. She was carrying a mug of
coffee. She looked enviously at the remains of Grimes'
breakfast, helped herself to a slice of toast and cream cheese.

She said plaintively, "I could pour myself a coffee but I
couldn't manage that machine . . ."

"I'll do you something, Shirl."

"Darleen. I've a sort of birthmark here . . ." She indicated
a mole on her upper thigh. "See."

"What about in the dark?" asked Grimes.

"You can feel it . . ."

She guided his hand to the spot.

"I'm *hungry*," complained Shirl, coming out to join them.
"I thought that passengers were supposed to be fed. I went up
to the . . . the control room to ask and they, the captain and
that Fenella, threw me out. They were . . ."

"I can guess," said Grimes.

He got up from the hatch and led the two girls into the
galley. They both wanted grilled fish for breakfast. (Whoever
that long-ago genetic engineer had been he had made considerable
modifications to the original stock; kangaroos are
herbivores.) They returned to the lazarette hatch, Grimes with
more coffee for himself. Sitting there in the warm sunlight
with an attractive girl on either side of him he was reminded
of a painting he had once seen. What was it called? Picnic On
The Grass, or something. But in that there was only one
naked woman, surrounded by fully clothed—even to tophats!
—men. Here it was a single clothed (more or less) man
surrounded by naked women.

And why should he be clothed? The air was warm and the
shirt, which should have been washed the previous night, was
uncomfortably sticky. He took it off. Darleen, on his right,
was sitting very close to him. So, on his left, was Shirl.

Shirl said, "I've a birthmark too, John . . ."

(Grimes wondered just how telepathic these women were.)

"Just under my left breast . . . If it's dark you can feel it . . ."

"It's not dark now," said Grimes, but allowed his hand to
be guided to the place. Somehow his fingers finished up on
her nipple—and the fingers of the hand that Darleen had
taken also strayed.

It was Darleen who fell back supine on to the hatch,

pulling Grimes with her. It was Shirl who found the fastening
at the waistband of his kilt, who pulled the garment from
him. He was the meat in an erotic sandwich, with Darleen's
moist, hungry mouth beneath his, with Shirl's breasts, with
their erect nipples, pressed into his naked back, with her teeth
gently nibbling his right ear.

From above there came laughter and the sound of hand-
clapping.

The girls would have ignored this but Grimes could not. He
extricated himself, not without difficulty, from the dual
embrace. He looked up. The obnoxious Onslow and the even
more obnoxious Fenella Pruin were at the rail at the after end
of the bridge, grinning down at them.

"Now you know what it's like to be interrupted!" said the
Pruin.

Twenty-nine

Grimes was used to odd voyages, to pleasant ones and to unpleasant ones. He was used (of course) to ships, although not at this stage of his career to vessels plying planetary seas rather than the oceans of deep space. But a ship is a ship is a ship, no matter in what medium she swims. Oars, sails, screw propellers, hydraulic jets, inertial drive units or whatever are all no more (and no less) than devices to move tonnage, small or considerable, from Point A to Point B fast or economically or, ideally, both.

Apart from the captain's quarters and the wheelhouse Grimes had the run of *Triton*. Onslow, infatuated with Fenella Pruin, let it be understood that his other passengers could look after themselves, preparing their own meals in the galley, signing for whatever liquor or cigars they took from the bar stores. Grimes did all the cooking for himself and Shirl and Darleen. He was used to getting the best out of an autochef, the two New Alicians were not. Anything they tried more complex than a simple grill was a culinary disaster.

Triton seemed to be navigating herself. Her pilot-computer had been programmed to keep her on a safe track along the coast, to compensate automatically for wind and current, to keep clear of other sea-borne traffic and, Grimes learned on one of the rare occasions that he met Onslow in the galley and had a brief conversation with him, to sound an alarm if the ship had gotten herself into a close quarters situation or any other potential danger.

Grimes, who spent most of the daylight hours on deck, watched the passing ships with interest. There were bulk carriers. There was an occasional huge cruise liner, white-gleaming with deck upon deck upon deck. There were fishing boats—some, dowdily utilitarian, obviously commercial, others so flashily painted and equipped that they must be catering to wealthy tourists wishing to combine their boozing and wenching with some outdoor sport.

Of these charter boats a few had what looked like a cannon

mounted forward. This intrigued Grimes; those little vessels could not possibly be warships. Then, one morning, he was privileged to see a gun in action. He watched, through borrowed binoculars, a harpoon streaking out to hit what, until the moment of impact had been no more than an almost totally submerged, immobile object that he had assumed was a waterlogged tree trunk.

There was more to it than had been visible above the surface, much more. The thing exploded in a frenzy of activity, thrashing the water in its agonies. There was a maned head at the end of a long, slender neck, there was a thick tail with flukes at the extremity, a barrel-shaped body with three pairs of flippers. After the initial flurry it sounded. The harpoon line stretched taut and the bows of the chaser almost went under. Then it was moving fast, under power, relieving the tension on the line as it pursued the stricken sea beast.

"They call them Moby Dicks," volunteered Darleen who, with Shirl, was standing with Grimes on the afterdeck.

"Moby Dicks? Couldn't they have found a name out of Greek mythology?" asked Grimes.

"What's that?" asked Shirl.

"Never mind. But what do they hunt them for? Are they good to eat?"

"No. But the tourists like sport—as *we* know."

"Too right," said Grimes.

"Even the Shaara hunt the Moby Dicks," said Darleen. "But they do it from their own airships. Their . . . blimps."

"They would," said Grimes. Then, reminiscently, "I used to think that the Shaara were a harmless, peace-loving people. I learned differently."

"They're only human," said Shirl.

"Mphm," grunted Grimes.

The chaser was hull down now, only its upperworks showing over the sea horizon. Grimes felt sorry for the Moby Dick. It had been basking on the surface, minding its own business and had been jerked into wakefulness by a harpoon, fired by some moneyed lout, in the guts. And after it had been messily slaughtered it would just be left drifting, to decompose . . .

He looked at his watch. It was almost lunchtime. He was beginning to feel hungry. The previous night, spent in the company of the New Alicians, eager to demonstrate the professional skills they had learned on New Venusberg, tolerant of the inadequacies engendered by past traumatic experiences and that he had yet fully to overcome, had been a wearing one.

* * *

Onslow was in the galley, setting the controls on the autochef, wearing the inevitable sarong. He looked pale under his tan. He, too, must have spent a wearing night.

He looked at Grimes, grinned weakly. "Good morning, Captain. Just fixing brunch for her ladyship. Just between ourselves, I shan't be sorry when this voyage is over . . ."

"When do we get there?" asked Grimes.

"Sixteen hundred hours tomorrow. You'll all have to keep out of sight while we're berthing, of course and not leave the ship until after dark. I've ironed all the details out with Fenella."

"I'm sure you have, Captain."

"And how's *your* ironing going on, Captain? Very nicely, by the looks of you."

"Mphm."

The gong sounded. Onslow unloaded a tray from the autochef. He said, "Be good. Don't do anything that you couldn't do riding a bicycle." He left Grimes to his own devices.

After a good lunch Grimes decided to take the sun on the deck above the wheelhouse while the two girls retired to their cabins for an afternoon nap. Although the wheelhouse itself was, so far as he knew, still out of bounds to passengers Onslow had made no mention of the monkey island. He took with him a box of cigarillos and some reading matter that he had found. Perhaps inevitably this consisted of a few dog-eared copies of *Star Scandals*. Among the other sensational stories there were a few by Fenella Pruin. In spite of the overwriting he found her account of life among the Blossom People on Francisco quite absorbing.

He became vaguely aware of a droning noise different from the subdued hum of *Triton*'s engines. He raised himself on his elbows, looked up and around. He saw it then, out to starboard, flying seaward from over the hazy coastline. It was a Shaara blimp.

He remembered being told that the Shaara hunted the things called Moby Dicks, using their own blimps rather than the charter chasers. And these must be Moby Dick waters; where there had been one there must be others. His sympathies lay with the victims of the chase rather than with the hunters but

he did almost hope that the arthropods would sight one of the
great beasts; he was curious to see how an airship would be
able to cope with the playing of a harpooned prey. And how,
he wondered, did the Shaara handle the recoil problem of the
harpoon gun?

At first it seemed that the airship was going to pass well
astern of *Triton* but it changed course, so as to fly directly
over her. That was natural enough. It was going nowhere in
particular and its crew might well be wanting a closer look at
the smart little surface vessel.

As it approached it lost altitude. That, too, was natural
enough. Grimes feeling mellow after his filling lunch with
rather too much chilled beer to wash it down, prepared to
forgive and to forget all the indignities he had suffered at the
hands of the Shaara, got to his feet and waved cheerfully.

He should have had more sense.

The blimp flew directly overhead. He could see Shaara
heads, with their antennae and huge, faceted eyes, peering
down from over the gunwale of the car. He could see, too,
the harpoon gun mounted forward, was interested to note that
it was a rocket launcher rather than a cannon proper. Then he
realised that nobody had answered his salutation.

Fuck 'em! he thought. *Snooty bee-bastards. Fuck 'em.*

The airship turned, coming around slowly. A Shaara, a
princess, thought Grimes, was standing beside the rocket
launcher working the laying wheel, depressing the launching
rack. The barbed head of the missile was pointing directly at
him.

Surely they wouldn't . . . he thought—and knew that they
would. He ran for the ladder on the starboard side of the
monkey island trying to get down to the bridge, to put the
wheelhouse between himself and the harpoon. He tripped on
the stack of magazines that he had brought up with him, fell
heavily. Half stunned, he was still trying to get to his feet
when the rocket was fired. He heard the swoosh of it and
thought, *This is it* . . .

Below him there was a screaming roar and a great crashing
and clattering. Working it all out later he came to the conclusion that some minor turbulence had caused the blimp's nose
to dip at the crucial moment so that the harpoon, missing
him, drove right through the wheelhouse, through the port
window and out through the starboard one. But at this moment all that mattered was that he was still alive. He wanted
to stay that way. He fell rather than clambered down the

starboard ladder to the bridge wing, trying to get to cover before the Shaara could reload. He hardly noticed the pain as his bare foot came down on a sharp-edged shard of plastic, part of the wreckage of the wheelhouse windows.

Then, automatically, his Survey Service training taking over, he began to assess damage. Looking into the wheelhouse he saw that the controls seemed to be undamaged. The harpoon must have plunged into the sea to starboard; its line, gleaming, enormously strong but light wire, was trailing aft. Grimes, who knew something about surface craft, wondered if he should stop the engines before the screw (or screws) got fouled. But *Triton,* with her hydraulic jet propulsion, had no external screws. Out to port the line, dipping in a graceful catenary, stretched to the blimp which was now running parallel to the surface ship. At the forward end of the car the figures of Shaara were busy about the rocket launcher, reloading it.

"What the hell's going on?" Onslow was roaring.

He had come up into his devastated wheelhouse, not bothering to dress, in his bewildered fury, his hairy nakedness, looking like the ancestral killer ape in person. He grabbed the taut harpoon line, shaking it viciously. He glared through the broken window at the blimp.

"Get under cover!" shouted Grimes. "They're going to fire again!"

"Two can play at that game!" yelled Onslow. He flung open the door of a locker on the after bulkhead of the wheelhouse, snatched from it a rifle. With the barrel he completed the destruction of the starboard window so that no remaining pieces of plastic obstructed his aim. He brought the butt of the weapon to his shoulder, sighted, fired. Grimes had expected that his target would be the Shaara who were now swinging the rocket launcher around to bear—but it was not. The burst of rapid fire was directed at the after end of the car, to the engine. Grimes saw the tracers strike, saw the coruscation of vividly blue sparks as broken circuits arced and fused. The pusher screw ceased to be a shimmering circle of near invisibility as the blades slowed and stopped. The airship dropped astern, still secured to *Triton* by the harpoon wire, being towed by her like a captive balloon.

"You should have gone for the gunners, Captain," Grimes told him. "They'll have us well within range as long as the wire holds . . ."

"And if I murder one of those murdering swine where will

I be? Behind bars—or in the Colosseum arena! They're rich, Grimes, *rich*—and justice, like everything else, is for sale on this world!" He grabbed Fenella—who had come up to the wheelhouse unnoticed until now—by the arm. "Here, now, make yourself useful! I taught you how to steer. Don't bother with a compass course. Just zig-zag . . ."

"Aren't you going to report this to the authorities, Captain?" asked Grimes.

"What with?" Onslow gestured towards the transceiver which was sited just below the sill of the starboard window. The harpoon itself had missed it but the line had sliced the box almost in two. "What with? Keep an eye on things up here while I go down to get tools to cut this blasted wire!"

His bare feet thudded heavily on the treads as he ran down the companionway.

Grimes took stock of the situation. Fenella—she had taken time to put on a sarong before coming up to the wheelhouse—was standing behind the binnacle, her hands on the two buttons used for manual steering. She pressed first one and then the other; the ship's head swung to port and to starboard obedient to the helm. She knew what was required; her alterations of course were sufficiently random to throw off the aim of any gunner not gifted with precognition.

She looked at him and grinned. "Boy! What a story I'll be writing!"

If you survive to write it, he thought but did not feel unduly pessimistic. He picked up the heavy rifle from where Onslow had put it down, went out to the starboard wing of the bridge. Shirl and Darleen, who had come up by an outside ladder, were there. Unlike Fenella they had not bothered to cover themselves. They were staring aft at the tethered blimp, dipping and yawing at the end of its long towline.

"What's doin'?" asked Shirl.

"They're after me," said Grimes. "The Shaara. It's an old grudge."

"After us too, like as not," said Darleen. "We killed four of the bastards in the Snuff Palace . . ."

The blimp's rocket projector fired. The missile fell into the sea at least half a kilometre on *Triton*'s starboard beam. Grimes laughed. Only a very lucky shot could hit the ship and the supply of harpoons must be limited. And once Onslow came up with something to cut the wire the Shaara would fall away rapidly astern, utterly impotent.

But what were they doing now?

First one dark shape dropped from the car, then another, then three more. Even at this distance Grimes could see the irridescent blur of their rapidly beating wings. They were overhauling *Triton* very slowly but they had less than two kilometres to fly and were, Grimes well knew, very strong fliers. Princesses, drones or worker-technicians? He could not tell. Armed or unarmed? The sunlight was reflected by something glitteringly metallic carried by one of them. A knife, possibly, or a handgun . . . But it didn't much matter. He, Grimes, had Onslow's rifle.

He checked the magazine.

It was empty.

He ran into the wheelhouse, to the locker from which the captain had taken the weapon. It was completely bare. But there must be some more ammunition somewhere.

Onslow came up from below, carrying a laser cutting torch.

"Where's your spare ammo?" asked Grimes.

"Haven't got any. This ain't a warship. Now, where do I cut this wire? It's going to lash back if I'm not careful . . . Now if I stand right in the middle of the wheelhouse to cut it I'll be safe, but the rest of you won't be. A spacer like you wouldn't know how a parted wire under a strain whips back . . ." (Grimes did know but this was no time to tell the other man.) "So either get below decks or up on monkey island." He patted Fenella's arse affectionately. "You're safe. You're right on the centreline."

"But the Shaara . . . They're coming after us. They'll be boarding shortly."

"They'll just have to wait till I've finished here. This harpoon wire is a bastard to cut through, even with laser . . ."

He switched on the pistol-like tool and the surface of the wire began to glow where the almost invisible beam impinged upon it.

Grimes ran out on to the bridge wing. He could not understand what the two New Alicians were doing. Stooping, the posture making their big rumps very prominent, they were gathering fragments of sharp-edged, shattered plastic from the deck, discarding some and keeping others.

"Get off the bridge!" he shouted. "This wire's going to go!"

They obeyed him but they did not run below, as he was expecting. They scampered up the ladder to monkey island. He followed them. They would be as safe from the flying

ends of wire there as anywhere else and would be able to see
what was happening.

Astern the blimp was still bobbing and weaving at the end
of its towline. The five Shaara who had left the crippled
airship were close now—two, the larger ones, princesses, the
other three drones. If the things that they were carrying had
been firearms they would have used them by now. Short
spears, Grimes decided. Probably the weapons used in the
final stages of the Moby Dick hunt—and such weapons could
be, would be used against him. Perhaps he should have run
below to find something with which to defend himself—a
spanner or hammer from the engineroom workshop, a knife
from the galley. But now it was too late. The wire must
surely be going to part at any moment and if he were on the
bridge when it did so he would be sliced in two.

Behind him and to either side of him Shirl and Darleen
shouted. He heard the whirring noise as the fragments of
flung plastic whirled past his head on either side, watched
their glittering trajectory. One struck the leading princess,
shearing off her iridescent wings at the left shoulder joint.
The other would have hit the drone flying beside her had he
not swerved and dipped. The injured Shaara fell to the sea,
legs and the remaining wings thrashing ineffectually.

Again the makeshift boomerangs were thrown. The other
princess was hit, but on the heavily furred thorax. She fal-
tered in her flight, falling behind the three drones, but kept on
coming. Grimes could see the spears clearly now, nasty
looking tridents. He picked up a shard of plastic, flung it
viciously. He gashed his hand but did no other damage while
Shirl, exhibiting far greater skill, decapitated a drone.

Then the wire parted. The end on the starboard side of the
wheelhouse, with the harpoon trailing from it, slid harmlessly
overside. The other end whipped up and back towards the
towed airship. The princess was in the way of it. The two
halves of her body plummeted to the water.

That left two drones.

These abandoned the chase, dropping to the sea to go to the
aid of the injured princess. The last that Grimes saw of them
they were flying slowly back to the drifting blimp, carrying
between them the body, possibly still living, of their superior.

Thirty

———◦●◦———

Triton came to Troy.

Her entrance into port was delayed; Onslow had not been able to notify the authorities of his impending arrival by radio telephone, the transceiver damaged by the Shaara harpoon being irreparable. So she had to lay off to seaward of the breakwaters while her captain tried to establish communication by daylight signalling lamp. His Morse was rusty, although no rustier than the Morse of the duty officer in the signal station. Finally he was able to find out where he was to berth and to order his linesmen; as *Triton* was crewless a mooring party would have to board as soon as she entered the harbour.

Grimes would have liked to watch the berthing procedure but he, with the three women, had to stay in his cabin until Onslow gave the all clear. So the four of them sat there waiting—Fenella in the single chair, Grimes between the two New Alicians on the bunk. The view from the port was very limited, affording only glimpses of cranes and gantries and, once, a huge bulk carrier.

They felt the bump as the launch with the mooring party came alongside. Then there was the vibration as the hydraulic jets were employed to give lateral thrust and, finally, another bump as *Triton*'s starboard side made contact with the wharf fendering. Not long after there was the sound of footsteps as two people came up the companionway from the poop deck. They passed through the passenger accommodation, carried on up to the captain's quarters.

Port officials? The ship's agent? Police?

The four of them sat there in silence. Fenella was smoking, one cigarillo after another. So was Grimes, although he would sooner have had a pipe. Shirl and Darleen did not smoke.

At last there was the sound of footsteps again. Three people were coming down the companionway. They did not pause on the passenger deck. After a short delay one person came on up, rapped sharply on the locked cabin door.

It had to be Onslow, thought Grimes as he opened up.

It was.

"The harbourmaster and my agent," reported the captain. "They wanted to know what the hell had happened to my wheelhouse. I told them the story that *you* cooked up, Fenella. They believed it." He laughed. "They'd have believed and liked the true story still more. They don't love the Shaara."

"My story is safer," Fenella Pruin said. "For all of us, you included. Don't forget that Grimes and I are officially dead until we elect to bob up again. You've never seen us, any of us. You were just steaming quietly along on your lawful occasions when a Moby Dick surfaced to starboard. Out to port there was this Shaara blimp with a hunting party. The trigger-happy bastards opened fire on their quarry, even though you were between it and them. Something went wrong and the harpoon went right through your wheelhouse, missing you by millimetres. You, looking after your own ship, decided to cut the wire—which had the harpoon, in the water, at one end of it and the blimp at the other. You did so. When you came out on deck you saw Shaara bodies in the water and a couple of drones picking one up. Some of them must have come out of the airship and were flying down to have a few words with you when the wire parted. A couple or three must have been caught by one of the ends when it whipped back . . ."

"Is that what you told them?"

"Yes."

"With no improvements of your own manufacture?"

"No."

"Good. If anybody else asks questions, stick to my version. I doubt very much if even the Shaara, arrogant insects that they are, would dare to admit to attacking a New Venusberg ship on the high seas. After all, they're the foreigners and you're the native . . ."

"*Native?*" asked Grimes.

"Clarry's naturalised," Fenella told him. "He had to be before he was allowed to command a New Venusberg ship." She turned to the shipmaster. "And now, how soon can we get out of here?"

"It'll be sunset in a couple of hours and there's not much twilight in these latitudes." He looked at her as he added, "I'll be rather sorry to see you go."

"I'm sure that you will."

Onslow transferred his attention to Grimes. "And who's going to pay for the repairs to my wheelhouse?"

"Your insurance," Grimes told him. "Or you can sue the Shaara."

"But if *you* hadn't been on board . . ."

"I paid my passage, which is more than somebody else did . . ."

"And I'm still paying *you*, Grimes, so shut up!" snapped Fenella Pruin. She said to the shipmaster, "Let's go up to your cabin, Clarry. It's a bit less crowded than here. We can talk things over there."

Plainly neither Grimes, Darleen nor Shirl was included in the "us". They remained sitting on the bunk while Onslow and Fenella Pruin left the cabin. Grimes hoped that they would make each other very happy.

They helped themselves to a last meal before leaving *Triton;* they did not know where the next one was coming from as, after paying the bar bill, Grimes had only a few credits left. They dressed in the clothing that, supplied by Onslow, was to be part of their disguise. (When captured and when escaping from the Snuff Palace none of them had been wearing sarongs.) Padded brassieres were contrived for Shirl and Darleen—"False upperworks!" laughed Onslow as he, personally, adjusted them on the girls' chests—as well as binding to reduce the size of their prominent rumps. From the neck down, at least, they no longer looked like New Alician women. Syntheskin from *Triton*'s medicine chest was used to gum Grimes' prominent ears flat to his skull. Onslow found a wig—it had been left behind by some past female passenger—for Fenella. It transformed her into a quite pretty redhead, somehow softened her features.

Grimes and the two Matilda's Children were first down the gangway. They waited on the wharf while Fenella and Captain Onslow made a last, passionate farewell on the poop deck. Her wig fell off. Grimes just caught it before it fell into the narrow gap between the ship's side and the wharf stringer.

At last she came down, took the artificial head covering from Grimes without a word of thanks, put it back on. She waved one last time to Onslow. Then, with Grimes in the lead they made their way to the Port Troy subway station. They kept away from the bright lights. This was easy as the only ship working cargo was a big bulk carrier. Apart from the activity about her the port area was very quiet. They met nobody during their short walk.

The entrance to the station was just an entrance, lacking

either crude or subtle sexual symbolism. There were no other intending passengers; the only similitude to life was that presented by the animated, pornographic advertisements to either side of the escalator and on the platform.

There was no through car to Port Aphrodite; they would have to change at New Bali Beach. That station was fairly busy. While they waited on the platform for the Port Aphrodite car Grimes felt uneasily that everybody was staring at them. He told himself firmly that this could not be so; their appearance was no more outré than that of the average tourist on this planet.

But there was one fat woman, herself sarong clad, who was subjecting Grimes, and Grimes only, to an intense scrutiny. He had seen her before somewhere, he thought.

But where?

When?

Then he remembered. She was one of the witnesses to his humiliation on Bali Beach when the Shaara had bombed him with garbage. She was the one whom he, rather childishly, had humiliated in her turn on the Platform of the Port Aphrodite subway station.

She approached him tentatively. She asked. "Isn't it Captain Grimes? I never forget a face . . ."

"My name, madam," said Grimes, "is Fenn." (It was the first one that came into his head. He realised that Fenella Pruin was glaring at him—but she did not hold a copyright on the alias.) He laughed. "I must have a double."

"I do beg your pardon, Mr Fenn. But you *are* like Captain Grimes—apart from your ears, that is. And I'm sorry, in a way, that you're not him . . ."

Is there a reward out? he wondered.

"Why?" he asked, trying to make his voice unconcerned.

"Because if you were him he'd still be alive. He was such a charming young man, in spite of his wealth so utterly unspoiled. There aren't many like him in the galaxy . . ."

"What do you mean, madam?" asked Grimes. "My friends and I are new here. We've yet to look at a newspaper or listen to a bulletin . . ."

"Oh, you must be passengers on that big ship that came in yesterday. I can't remember her name but my hubby, who used to be in shipping—on the business side, of course—told me that she's one of the Commission's Beta Class liners under new ownership. But this Captain Grimes is—or was, but they haven't found any bodies yet although they found wreckage—a shipowner as well as being a space captain. Only a little ship but built, so they say, of gold. I can't believe that but she shines like gold. He came here with just one passenger, a girl as rich as himself. They chartered one of those camperflies and flew off for a tour. They never came back. They were last seen taking off from Vulcan Island. Pilot error it must have been, although you'd think that a man who could take a spaceship all around the galaxy would be able to manage a *camperfly*. Even my hubby can, although he's certainly not either a spaceman or an airman. He just sets the controls on automatic and presses the buttons for where he wants to go. Perhaps that was the trouble. Would a *real* captain be happy to let his ship do his thinking for him?

"And then, of course, he had a beautiful young lady with him . . . Perhaps, when he should have been piloting, he was doing something else. I don't want to speak ill of the dead but the girl—what was her name?—was free with her favours. There was that fat Port Captain for one; I did hear that he actually burst into tears when he heard that his lady love was missing . . . Now what was *her* name? It's on the tip of my tongue. Prudence something or other—but she wasn't very prudent, was she?

"No, what am I thinking about? Not Prudence. Prunella. Yes, that was it. Prunella . . .? Prunella Fenn. You wouldn't be her brother, would you? Or perhaps her husband, come here to find out what happened to her . . .?"

"No," said Grimes. "No relation."

"But what a coincidence! You looking like Captain Grimes—but much better looking!—and with the same name as the young lady who was with him when he vanished . . ."

Fortunately the Port Aphrodite car came in. Grimes practically shoved his three companions through the open door into the interior. He paused briefly to say, "Thank you for the talk, madam." He laughed. "After what you've told us *we* shan't be hiring a camperfly! A very good night to you."

The door closed before he had taken his seat. The car sped through the tunnel.

"Did you have to use Fenn as a name?" asked Fenella coldly.

"It's as good as any other," said Grimes. "Or is it? Anyhow, we've learned a bit. We—you and I, that is, Fenella—are definitely missing, presumed dead. Your fat friend Jock is heartbroken. He'll be overjoyed to see you again. You—we—

had better concoct a story to satisfy him. We'll probably need his help to get back on board *Little Sister*."

"All right, Mr *Fenn*. What are *your* ideas?"

"You're the writer."

"Not a fiction writer."

"No?" He raised his eyebrows, winced as this caused a sting of pain in the skin of his skull under his gummed down ears. "No? Judging from some of your pieces that I read in *Star Scandals* . . ."

"None of them," she told him, "more fantastic than the story of what's happened to us on this world."

Thirty-one

No other passengers boarded the car at the two stops before arrival at Port Aphrodite. Grimes and Fenella were able to work out the details of what they hoped would be a plausible story. It did not tally with the one that Captain Onslow had told the authorities in Troy but, hopefully, *Little Sister* would be well up and away from New Venusberg before there was any thorough checking up.

They would tell Captain McKillick that they had visited Vulcan Island in the rented camperfly. Returning to the mainland they had seen, on the surface, a huge sea beast, a Moby Dick. Fenella Pruin—Prunella Fenn, rather—had wanted a closer look at the monster. They had been flying only a few metres above it when it had lashed up and out with its tail, which had done the aircraft no good at all. It had crashed into the water and broken up.

Grimes and Fenella had gotten away, using one of the camperfly's wings as a raft. (Although the gas cell was holed there was still sufficient buoyancy for it to stay afloat.) They had drifted on to a small island and had stayed there, living on fruit and roots and shellfish, until they had been fortunate enough to attract the attention of the passing *Triton*. Then, during the voyage to Troy, there had been another unfortunate incident. Grimes, sunbathing on the upper deck, had been recognised by one of the crew—probably that princess whom he had first met in Lady Luck's—of a Shaara blimp on a Moby Dick hunting expedition. This spiteful being had taken a shot at him with the blimp's rocket harpoon. She had missed Grimes but scored a hit on *Triton*'s wheelhouse. When the wire had parted an end of it, whipping back, had killed or injured a few hapless Shaara who had left their airship to make an assessment of the situation.

It was decided that Fenella would try to call *Triton*, from a public call box, as soon as they got to Port Aphrodite. Onslow had told her that he intended to have his damaged transceiver replaced that night; in fact the technicians had been due on board only half an hour or so after the fugitives had left the ship. The captain would then be able to amend his story to make it agree with theirs.

The car arrived at the Port Aphrodite station.

There were people on the platform awaiting the transport to carry them to various pleasure establishments. None of these was at all interested in Grimes and his three companions. There were public call boxes at the head of the escalator. There were a few moments of panic when Grimes could not find the much depleted notecase that he had tucked into the waistband of his sarong. While he was fumbling it fell to the floor between his feet. He picked it up, gave it to Fenella.

She went into the box. Grimes and the two New Alicians watched her through the transparent door and walls as she fed one of the plastic bills into the slot. The screen lit up, showing the face—that of a silver woman—of the roboperator. Fenella said something. The robot replied, the metallic lips moving mechanically. There was a short delay. Then the original picture in the screen faded, was replaced by one of the bearded face of Captain Onslow. He was not alone; there was a brief glimpse of a head of luxuriant blonde hair in the background, of smooth, sun-tanned skin. *A girl in every port,* thought Grimes amusedly, *as well as girls between ports wherever possible* . . .

Onslow did not seem at all pleased to be seeing and hearing his recent lady love so soon after the fond farewell. His initial scowl, however, was replaced by a somewhat spurious smile. He said little, let Fenella do most of the talking. He looked relieved when the conversation was terminated.

Fenella came out of the box. She seemed amused rather than otherwise. She said, "He didn't waste much time, did he? Off with the old love, on with the new . . . Just one of those things . . ."

"Shits that pass in the night," said Grimes.

"*Very* funny!" she snapped. "Very funny. Well. Anyhow, he's agreed to change his story the next time that anybody asks him how his wheelhouse got busted up. I didn't have much trouble persuading him. He was wanting to get back to that brazen floosie he had with him."

"Mphm."

"And now let's get back to *your* precious ship."

They left the station, walked out into the soft night. The spaceport was almost as it had been when they left it. There were two freighters working cargo with glaring lights all about them. There were the cruise liners. There was *Little Sister*, goldenly agleam in her berth between two big ships. One was the Shaara vessel that had been there when they arrived. The other was one of the Interstellar Transport Commission's Beta Class passenger liners. But was she still owned by the Commission? A flag, softly floodlit, flew from the telescopic mast extruded from her sharp stem, an ensign of imperial purple with, in glowing gold, the CR monogram, the symbol representing the Credit, the galaxy-wide monetary unit.

It was the flag of El Dorado.

And why not? The El Doradans, Grimes well knew, enjoyed kinky sex as much as anybody and could afford to pay for it better than most.

But the name of the ship . . .

He could read it now, in golden (of course) letters on the burnished grey shellplating under the control room.

Southerly Buster III . . .

Southerly Buster . . . Drongo Kane . . .

And Kane, through his Able Enterprises, pulled far heavier Gs on New Venusberg than Grimes or even Fenella Pruin.

He said as much to her as they walked towards *Little Sister*. She agreed with him but said that it was of no consequence; once they got off this cesspit of a planet she would lift the lid off the whole, stinking can of worms.

There were guards around *Little Sister*—not only a Customs officer but two armed men in uniform—modelled on that of the Federation Marines—of the spaceport police.

One of these said sharply, "Halt! I'm sorry, gentlepersons, but nobody is allowed near this ship."

"I am the master," said Grimes, with deliberate pomposity. "I am Captain Grimes."

"*If* you are," said the guard, "you don't look anything like your photograph. Captain Grimes has *ears*. Yours are quite normal."

"The airlock door is coded to me," said Grimes. "It will let me in."

"I'm sorry, sir. My orders are that nobody, but nobody, is to approach this ship."

"But I am Captain Grimes. I am the master. The owner."

"So *you* say, sir."

"I am Prunella Fenn," said Fenella Pruin.

"Somebody else who doesn't look much like her photograph!" laughed the guard.

"Captain McKillick will soon identify me—but I most certainly do not wish to be kept hanging around until tomorrow morning!"

"You can see the Port Captain now, lady. He is in his office, still. Some business over the El Doradan ship."

"All right," she said. "We'll see him now. And you'll soon find out who we are."

McKillick, as the guard had said, was in his office. Apart from those with whom he was discussing business the administration block was empty; there was nobody to detain Grimes and the three women on their way up to the top floor.

The office door opened silently as they approached it. The Port Captain, studying papers spread over his desk, did not notice. Neither did the two people, a man and a woman, sitting in chairs facing him. The man was wearing a purple uniform with heavy golden epaulettes. The woman was clad in translucent white beneath which her body glowed goldenly. Diamonds glittered in the braided coronet of her glossy auburn hair, in the pendants hanging from her ears.

"As far as I know," the fat McKillick was saying, "Captain Grimes and his passenger, Prunella Fenn, were lost when their hired camperfly crashed in the sea shortly after lifting off from Vulcan Island. I blame myself for the tragedy. I should never have allowed them to leave Port Aphrodite. Grimes I did not trust. The man was no more than an adventurer, battening on wealthy women . . ."

"Captain Grimes," said the woman coldly, "was—or is—an extremely competent shipmaster."

"Be that as it may," went on McKillick, "that camperfly did crash in the sea. A search was made but only the wreckage of the aircraft was found. The cause of the disaster could only have been pilot error."

"Indeed?" the woman said. "The story that *we* heard, in a Carlottigram from Captain Dreeble of *Willy Willy*, was a rather different one. That camperfly may or may not have crashed—but Captain Grimes wasn't in it. At this moment he's probably one of the star attractions at the Colosseum—if he's still alive, that is. He had better be."

"He will be," growled her companion. "His famous luck more than compensates for his many shortcomings."

"Mphm," grunted Grimes indignantly.

McKillick lifted his eyes from the papers on his desk. He stared at Grimes and the three women. The purple-uniformed man and his companion swivelled around in their chairs, also stared.

"Grimes . . ." murmured Drongo Kane at last. "Live, on stage, in person. Singing and dancing. But what's happened to your ears?"

"Grimes . . ." said the Baroness. "Grimes. I was very worried when Commodore Kane got that message about you from Captain Dreeble, especially when he told me about the Colosseum. I'd no idea—believe me, John, I had no idea—what sort of entertainments are available on this planet . . ."

"Grimes!" shouted McKillick. "Grimes! But who are those people with you? What did you do to Prue?" He was on his feet, looking as though he were about to clamber over his desk to shake the truth out of *Little Sister*'s captain. "Where is she? Tell me, damn you, where is she?"

"Here," said Fenella.

"But . . . You?"

She snatched off her disguising wig.

"Prue! You're safe! You're safe!" McKillick did not clamber over his desk but ran clumsily around it. He threw his arms about her, pulled her to him in a bear-like hug. Her face wrinkled in distaste.

"Very touching," remarked Drongo Kane, his carelessly assembled features under the straw-coloured hair creased in a sardonic smile. Then, to the Baroness, "I told you that Grimes would muddle through, as usual, Micky."

Fenella Pruin managed to extricate herself from McKillick's embrace. "Later, Jock," she said. "Later." Then, to Grimes, "This appears to be some sort of reunion as far as you're concerned. Would you mind doing the introductions?"

"Er, yes, Fenella—sorry, Prunella—may I present you to the Baroness Michelle d'Estang of El Dorado?"

"Am I supposed to curtsey?" asked Fenella.

The Baroness looked at her disdainfully. "You may if you wish."

"And to Captain Drongo Kane . . ."

"You've got it wrong, cobber," said that gentleman. "It's Commodore Baron Kane, of the El Doradan Navy."

"Commanding a merchant ship," sneered Grimes. "A cruise liner. A spaceborne gin palace."

Kane laughed. "A cruise liner she may be—but she's rated as an auxiliary cruiser. But who are those two sheilahs with you?"

"Shirl," said Shirl.

"Darleen," said Darleen.

"New Alicians, ain't you, with those faces and accents? Matilda's Stepchildren. What are two nice girls like you doing mixed up with Grimes and this muckraking news hen?"

"Muckraking news hen?" asked McKillick bewilderedly.

"Didn't you know, Captain? This is Fenella Pruin, the pride and joy of some local rag on her home planet and the even greater pride and joy of *Star Scandals*. It wouldn't at all surprise me if you were one of her Faithful Readers. She's just been using you, the same as she's used men on hundreds of worlds. She's all set and ready to spill all the unsavoury beans about New Venusberg."

"And what about you, Commodore or Baron or whatever you call yourself?" she shouted. "What about *your* interests here? Your nasty little slave trade from New Alice to the New Venusberg brothels—and worse!"

"Slave trade, my dear? But the New Alicians are underpeople, have no more rights than animals. The ships that bring them here are cattle ships, not slave ships."

"Are they? *Are they?* Wasn't it ruled, some many years ago, that underpeople are to be reclassified as human as long as interbreeding between them and true humans is possible?"

"In this case it ain't, Miss Pruin. It's obviously impossible. The ancestors of the New Alicians were marsupials, not placental mammals."

"Their *ancestors*, Mr Kane. And, in any case, I imagine that the crews of your slave ships—sorry, cattle ships—aren't too fussy about having intercourse with them."

"Of course not. I don't recruit my personnel from Sunday schools."

"You can say that again. But I have seen—I'm not telling you where—a New Alician boy who bears a very strong resemblance to his father. To *your* precious Captain Dreeble."

Kane laughed, although he looked uneasy. "I've often entertained doubts about Dreeble's own ancestry," he said.

Grimes laughed. "Morrowvia all over again, isn't it?"

"So the New Alicians are legally human," remarked the Baroness. "So what? All that we have to do is get them to sign proper contracts. What does worry me is that Captain Grimes' current inamorata—I've noticed before that he has the most deplorable taste in women!—is all set and ready to make a big splash in her gutter rag about New Venusberg. Once again—so what?

"El Dorado has big money invested in this world and I,

speaking for my fellow El Doradans, shall welcome the free
advertising that New Venusberg will be getting. But . . .'' she
turned to Kane . . . ''there will have to be a thorough
housecleaning. I did not know of the existence of such establishments as the Colosseum and the Snuff Palace until you
told me.'' Suddenly there was icy contempt in her voice.
With pleasure Grimes saw that she was making Kane squirm
as, so often during the days aboard *The Far Traveller*, she
had made him squirm. *''You* thought that it was a great joke
that Grimes would end his days slaughtered in the arena. We
are two of a kind, I know—but only up to a point. And
beyond that point I refuse to pass. There will be a thorough
investigation of the state of affairs on New Venusberg—but
without overmuch publicity.''

''Yes, Micky,'' said Kane.

McKillick was at last able to make himself heard. ''Prunella!''
he bleated to Fenella Pruin. ''How could you have done
this to *me?* You—a spy!''

''The name is Fenella Pruin,'' she told him coldly.

''But, Prunella . . .''

The Baroness interrupted. ''Port Captain, will you expedite
the Outward Clearance of *Little Sister?* Get the necessary
officials, Port Health, Customs and the like, out of their beds,
or whatever beds they happen to be occupying. Captain Grimes
isn't safe on this planet and I want him off it. Rightly or
wrongly he will be blamed for the upheaval that will soon
take place.''

''What about consumable stores?'' asked Grimes.

A tolerant smile softened the Baroness's patrician features.
''You haven't changed, John. Even though you no longer
have Big Sister to pamper you I imagine that you make sure
that you never starve.''

''Too right,'' said Grimes.

While they were talking they drifted towards the door,
which opened for them, out of the office, into the corridor.
He could hear, faintly, the voices from inside the room—
Drongo Kane at his hectoring worst, McKillick pitifully
bleating, Fenella Pruin emitting an occasional outraged scream.
Shirl and Darleen did not seem to be making any contribution
to the argument. But he was no longer interested. He was too
conscious of the close proximity of that filmily clad body to
his. He could smell what once had been, during his tour of__
duty as captain of her spaceyacht, her familiar scent, cool yet
warm, sensual yet unapproachable.

She said, "At times—not all the time, but increasingly so—I'm sorry that Captain Kane turned up when he did. Just when we, alone in the pinnace, were about to do what we'd been putting off for far too long . . ." She put her slender hands on his shoulders, turned him to face her, regarded him with what he realised was affection. "You're an awkward brute at times, for most of the time, but there's something about you. An integrity. I'm fond of Peter, of course . . ." (*Peter?* wondered Grimes. But "Drongo" was probably not Kane's given name.) "I'm fond of Peter—in a way. He's masterful, which I like, but rather too ruthless at times. And he thought that it was a huge joke when he received that message from Aloysius Dreeble—that poisonous little rat! —telling him that you'd been condemned to the Colosseum. (It was only then that I learned that there was such an establishment on this world.) I persuaded him to cancel the ship's visit to New Sparta and to make all possible speed here to try to save you, if it were not too late . . .

"But, of course, you'd already saved yourself."

"With assistance, Michelle."

"Perhaps. But I'm sure that *she*, that muckraker, wasn't much help. It must have been those others, with the horse faces and the ugly names . . . There's a certain strength about them . . ."

"And they throw a wicked boomerang," said Grimes.

"I wish I could have seen it." She laughed softly. "And there's another thing I'd like to see. Again. *The Far Traveller*'s pinnace. I like the name that you gave her—*Little Sister*. And we have unfinished business aboard her, don't we?"

Grimes remembered well that unfinished business—when he, naked, had been holding the naked Michelle in his arms, when the preliminaries to their lovemaking (never to be resumed) had been interrupted by the obnoxious voice of Drongo Kane from the Carlotti transceiver.

He said, "She's under guard. The guards wouldn't let me board her."

"They will," she said, "when I tell them to . . . Come."

They seemed to have stopped arguing in the Port Captain's office. As Grimes and the Baroness turned to make their way to the escalator the door opened. Drongo Kane emerged, scowling. He glared at Grimes.

"Ah, there you are. Well, Micky, orders have gone out that the Colosseum and the Snuff Palace are to be closed down immediately, pending a full enquiry. Of course, you realise that this is going to play hell with our profits. *Your* profits as well as mine."

She said, "There are more things in life than money."

"Name just two!" he snarled. Then, to Grimes, "This is all your doing. As usual. I thought that at long last you'd be out of my hair for keeps—but Her Highness here had to shove her tits in!"

There was a noise like a projectile pistol shot as the flat of her hand struck Kane's face. He stood there, rubbing the reddened skin—and then, surprisingly, he smiled. Even more surprisingly it was not a vicious grin.

He said, admiringly, "I always did like a woman with spirit, Micky."

"There are times," she told him coldly, "when a woman with spirit finds it very hard to like you." She addressed Grimes, "I think that the sooner you're off the planet the better. I can't guarantee your safety. Or that of your companions. Not only will the proprietors of some of the establishments here be gunning for you but there is also my . . . consort, who never has liked you." She allowed a small smile momentarily to soften her features. "But I should imagine that you are already aware of that."

"I shall want stores before I go," said Grimes.

"Then you're out of luck," Drongo Kane said smugly. "McKillick was able to arrange your Outward Clearance but, at this time of night, it was impossible to find a ship chandlery open."

"That presents no problem," the Baroness said. *"Southerly Buster* is well stocked with everything. Peter, will you see to it that what is necessary is transferred from your ship to Captain Grimes' vessel?"

"Am I a philanthropic institution?" bellowed Kane.

"Perhaps not. But *I* am the major shareholder in your Able Enterprises."

"All right," grumbled Kane. "All right. And as for you, Grimes, I suggest that you and your popsies get your arses aboard your little boat while they're still intact."

"Pinnace," corrected Grimes stiffly.

"Or lugger, if you like. Once aboard the lugger and the girls are yours. But not *my* girl." He put a possessive arm about the Baroness's waist.

She disentangled herself, turned to face Grimes. She was as tall as he and did not have to hold her face up to be kissed—and the kiss was not a light one.

"Goodbye, John," she said. "Or *au revoir* . . ."

"Break it up, Micky," snarled Kane. And to Grimes, "It's time that I didn't have to look at you!"

"Goodbye, John," said the Baroness again. "Look after yourself, and those two nice girls. As for the other one—I shall want a few words with her before she joins you aboard *Little Sister*."

Shirl and Darleen were already in the corridor, watching and listening with interest. Fenella Pruin was still in the office, no doubt saying her farewell to Captain McKillick. The Baroness, followed by Kane, went back into the Port Captain's sanctum. It was not long before he heard, through the closed door, Fenella Pruin's indignant screams. She seemed to be very annoyed about something.

But he could not distinguish what was being said and he wanted to get back aboard his ship to see that all was in order. With the two New Alicians, one on either side of him, he made his way out of the administration block. The guards at his airlock must have been told to allow him through. They saluted him smartly, stood aside.

Back in *Little Sister* he felt much happier. He checked everything. Apart from the legal formalities he could be ready to lift off within minutes. Even the stores were of no great importance provided that one was willing to put up with a monotonous diet.

Fenella Pruin came aboard.

She was crestfallen, sullen. She glowered at Grimes.

"*Your* friends!" she spat. "Her Exalted Highness the Baroness of Bilge! And the Lord High Commodore! Ptah!"

"He's no friend of mine," said Grimes. "Never has been."

"But she is. And that's not all. She's a major shareholder in Star Scandals Publishing. So . . ."

"So what?"

"Do I have to spell it out for you? Are you as dim as you look? She put the pressure on. I shall be graciously permitted to write a story, a good story even but nothing like as good as it should have been. I shall have to keep both feet firmly on the soft pedal. She laid down the guidelines. For example: 'Due to an unfortunate misunderstanding Captain Grimes and I were arrested and sentenced to a term in a punishment and rehabilitation centre for vicious criminals. We were released,

with apologies, as soon as our identities were established
. . .' '' She laughed bitterly. "Ha! Ha bloody ha!"

"But things are going to be cleaned up here," said Grimes.
"Such establishments as the Colosseum are going to be closed
down. And that's more important than your story."

"Is it? Is it? And how do you know, anyhow?"

"She promised."

"And you believed her?"

"Yes," said Grimes firmly.

Thirty-two

───────◆───────

There was somebody at the outer airlock door wanting admittance.

It was a supercilious young El Doradan officer in purple uniform, a single gold band on each of his sleeves. He looked curiously at the women, his expression conveying the impression that he had seen much better. He looked with disapproval at Grimes' informal sarong, asked, "You *are* the captain?"

"I have that honour," said Grimes, blinking at the other's purple and gold resplendence. He looked hard at the young man's face, was both relieved and disappointed when he could find there was no resemblance to himself. His own son, of whom the Princess Marlene was the mother, would be about the age of this youngster.

"Commodore Kane told me to find out what consumable stores you will be requiring. Sir."

"Come through to the galley while I make a check . . ." The officer followed Grimes into the little compartment. "Mphm . . . Would you have any pork tissue culture in your vats? And we shall be needing fresh eggs. And bacon . . . And coffee. And table wines, of course . . ."

The young man took notes. His manner toward Grimes oscillated between almost contemptuous disapproval and respect. After all, he was an El Doradan and therefore to him Money was one of the many Odd Gods of the Galaxy—and *Little Sister*, in her construction and appointments, reeked of Money. If only her captain had the decency to dress the part . . .

A Customs officer, a surly, middle-aged woman obviously rudely awakened from her much-needed beauty sleep, came on board with papers for Grimes to sign. He put his name to them, wondering as he did so who had paid *Little Sister*'s port dues. He had not and had no intention of doing so unless compelled. He asked the woman to unseal the locker in which the small arms and the crystals from the laser cannon had been stowed. She complied with his request reluctantly, tell--

ing him sternly that he was not to replace the crystals until he was off New Venusberg. He examined the pistols. They were in order. It was ironical that he had weapons now that the need for them (he hoped) was gone.

The stores were brought aboard from *Southerly Buster*. The young officer handed Grimes a parcel, wrapped in parchment and tied with a golden ribbon, said, "With Her Excellency's compliments, sir."

Grimes opened it. There were two large tins of tobacco and, in its own case, a beautiful brier pipe.

"Thank Her Excellency for me, please," he said.

"Certainly, sir." The young man smiled unpleasantly. "And the commodore asked me to say that he hopes it chokes you."

"You can tell Commodore Kane, from me, to . . . Oh, skip it. He knows what I think about him."

Grimes went into the galley, supervised the two stewards in their stowage of the various items, put the pork into the cooler until such a time as a vat could be readied for its reception. He followed them back into the cabin. They wished him *bon voyage* and went out through the airlock. The officer saluted stiffly, then left *Little Sister*.

Fenella Pruin looked at Grimes, looked at Shirl and Darleen.

"Well?" she asked.

"Well what?" countered Grimes.

"Aren't you going to say your fond farewells?" she demanded.

"To whom?"

"Those two."

"They're coming with us," said Grimes.

"*What?*"

"Of course. What will their lives be worth if we leave them here? They're wanted for a few murders, you know. And we were accessory to some of those killings."

"Always the space lawyer, aren't you? I know something about the law myself, Grimes. I would remind you that I am chartering this ship."

"Your employers are."

"And *I* decide what passengers may or may not be carried."

"Her Excellency," said Grimes, "is your employer, as you discovered this evening. She charged me to look after Shirl and Darleen. She didn't as much as mention *you*, by the way."

He brushed past her, stamped forward to the control cab,

sat down firmly in the pilot's seat. He turned to look aft into the main cabin. He could see Fenella, in profile. She was glaring at Shirl and Darleen. They were staring back at her defiantly. He pushed the button on the control panel that closed the airlock doors, sealed the ship. He said into the microphone of the NST transceiver, *"Little Sister* to Aerospace Control. Request permission to lift ship."

"Permission granted, *Little Sister."*

The voice was familiar. Yes, that was McKillick's fat face in the screen of the transceiver.

There was no *bon voyage.* There were no pleasantries whatsoever. If looks could have killed Grimes would have died at his controls.

The inertial drive grumbled and *Little Sister* detached herself from the concrete, rose vertically. To one side of her was the towering *Southerly Buster,* to the other the great, metallic skep that was the Shaara ship. There was activity in this latter's control room; Grimes could see huge, faceted eyes peering at him through the viewports. He wondered briefly what their owners were thinking. But for all their wealth and influence they were only tourists on this planet. The real power lay with human capitalists, of whom the Baroness was one. Once he had almost—at least!—hated her but, now, he both respected and trusted her. He had no doubt that the worst abuses on New Venusberg would be put a stop to.

Just in time he turned to look out and down to *Southerly Buster.* There was a white-clad figure in the big ship's control room, one hand raised in a gesture of farewell. He lifted his own arm in reply, hoped that she would see. Then *Little Sister* was high above the spaceport. In the keel viewscreens were the toylike ships and buildings, the dwindling, floodlit form of the wantonly asprawl White Lady. A lot had happened since he first set eyes on that piece of pornographic landscape gardening.

"Goodbye, *Little Sister,"* said McKillick. "Don't come back."

"If I do," said Grimes, "it will be fifty years too soon.

He heard the sound of quarrelling female voices behind him.

This would not be, he predicted to himself, one of the more pleasant voyages of his career.

But it would be interesting.